Afterglow

Elizabeth Walker

Published by Elizabeth Walker, 2020.

This is a work of fiction. Similarities to real people, places, or events are entirely coincidental.

AFTERGLOW

First edition. June 3, 2020.

Copyright © 2020 Elizabeth Walker.

ISBN: 979-8223833970

Written by Elizabeth Walker.

CHAPTER 1 - MARK

I DON'T LIKE MY CONDO. It's the windows. They're enormous, stretching from floor to ceiling, from one end of the bedroom to the other. Letting all the light in the world in. Sure, it's stylish, and it's what Tara wanted, but I never ever really sleep as much as I want to. All light, all the time. If it's not the city lights flickering in the dead of night, it's the sun rising in the morning. I can't remember the last time I slept in. Can't remember the last time I had one of those impeccable days where I just lie in and enjoy the warmth and comfort of my bed.

Work has been killing me lately, and it will continue to kill me for the next few months at least. Hence my despondency over not being able to sleep in. Especially on a weekend like this. It's been a tiring few weeks, and there's only going to be more things to do in the future. A new hire starting tomorrow. Clients already on edge. New tech builds. The whole marketing process tightening like a noose around my neck.

Okay. Maybe it's not entirely the light and the windows that are at fault here. Hell, Tara's been complaining about me grinding my teeth in the middle of the night. Now I can't get out of bed. My get up and go has has got up and left, as they say. Lazy Sunday.

"Okay guys! That's me, signing off! Remember to like and subscribe, and I'll have a video for you soon!" Tara says as she pads down the small entrance hallway of the condo, in full-on selfie-video mode. She's working hard. This early in the morning. On a Sunday. A quick little "bloop" and the app is turned off. I hope. I don't want any of her fans seeing me all blobbed out in bed. It wouldn't help her influencer image one bit.

It's not my thing, and sometimes I *really* can't stand it ever since she turned a corner of the condo into a mini-studio with lights and a screen, but even I can't deny that Tara's very good at the whole vlogging and modelling thing she does. Three-point-five million followers can't be wrong. Our postbox stuffed with free samples and companies wanting her sponsorships can't be wrong. She's on her way, and she's told me that there's no way this train is slowing down. Which is fine. I think.

"Babe, are we going still going out for dinner tonight?" she asks as she throws her phone down on the bed next to me and climbs over the thick duvet top for a snuggle. I'm roused from my general malaise.

"Yeah, if you want. What were you thinking?" I ask. She shrugs. I remember the last time we went out, someone recognized her, and it left her buzzing the whole night. I remember just really wanting my privacy.

"Anywhere, I guess. Oh. No, wait. No pasta. It makes me bloated and I have some yoga pants and sports bra videos to do tomorrow. I can't look all gross." I wanted pasta, but I keep my mouth shut.

"Maybe takeout?" I ask. "We could just stay in?"

"Hrm, maybe. It's supposed to get really nice out later though." A glance at the endless grey clouds and the dull silver light that's bathing everything doesn't really highlight that possibility. Yeah, I'm being grumpy.

"We can do that," I say. "I'm easy."

"I know, that's why I love ya, Mark," she says, laying a warm kiss on my cheek. "You're low-maintenance."

"Hrm," I grumble, faux-irritated.

Tara curls into me, her leg moving over my torso, her hand going to my bare chest. I'm naked under the comforter. She's been working all morning and I'm just, I don't know, sort of here. Not even bothering to get dressed.

Her skinny leg pressing against my groin as my arm goes around her. She's small, angular, easy to hold. I practically tower over her, even next to her in bed. It's an okay, comfortable feeling. I met her through my friend's aunt, strangely enough. She seemed happy, and had a vision about how she wanted to take her "brand", and was very driven and perky in everything she did. It was extremely easy to fall for her.

A year ago, when we started living together, that all seemed fairly admirable. My company had built one of the apps she's so popular on. Great and good. Nothing wrong about that. A symbiotic relationship.

She starts lightly kissing my neck, giggling into me. I can see where this is starting to go. I guess staying in bed wasn't too bad of an idea.

"Are you sure you can't do pasta?" I ask, hopeful. "Even just a little bit of it? I'm really feeling like it tonight. Hell, I'll even make some." My cooking skills are probably average at best. I have no idea why I thought I could swing that as a dealbreaker. She shakes her head, keeps kissing me, little pecks on my neck and cheek.

"Can't. Sorry. You know what people will say if I have a gut or something. They'll think I'm pregnant, or say mean things. I can't deal with any of that. No gossip for me, please."

"No problem. Not a big deal. I totally get it." It really isn't a big deal at all. Like she said, I'm low-maintenance, but having conversations like this always leaves me feeling weird. I'm still not used to it. "It's sponsored content, and people will be looking extra close. I get it."

"I know you do, babe," she says, kissing me on the cheek. I can feel her smile pressed up against me. "Hey, want to see a little preview of the new clothes I get to wear in my video tomorrow?" She asks me in a whisper, right in my ear. Her hand resting on my chest goes a little lower, to my stomach. Her fingertips trail my abs. "It might take your mind off all your worky-work."

Her hand reaches below the blanket.I can feel her finger tips grazing my cock lightly, feel that familiar stir when she touches me like that.

"Okay, go for it," I tell her. I kiss her deeply, wrap my arms around her momentarily in a warm embrace. I kiss her neck, near her chin. Right where I know she likes it. I very briefly think about giving her a hickey, but that would another video violation on the level of the pasta. My hands go to her cute little butt, squeezing and pulling her closer to my growing hard-on. I can feel how firm and small her ass is in my hands. She shivers a bit, goosebumps raising on her arms.

"I'm going to *love* showing off for you," she moans in my ear, and very, very reluctantly pushes away from me. I can tell, because she's slow about it. Normally she's all quick, strong movements, small punctuations of motion. She climbs out of the tangle of my arms and the comforter, getting up off the bed as I turn to watch her walk over to her dresser, which is right next to the windows in the corner of our room. She's already in yoga clothes, so it seems a little silly that she'll just be changing into other ones, but right now, I'm not complaining.

She pulls the small, fresh fabric out of the top drawer, and looks over her shoulder at me, coquettish and flirty. She's nimble, skinny, with blonde-dyed hair tied loosely in a ponytail. A ballerina's body. In one fluid motion, she bends over in front of me and pulls her yoga pants down.

No panties on. Her inviting slit between her legs. Familiar and a lot of fun.

She turns and we share smiles. She bites her lip as she presents herself to me, and I can feel myself getting even harder as I get a good look at her. Slowly, but surely she gets the new yoga pants on. These ones are light grey compared to the pink ones she was previously in. She shimmies into the pants, bouncing every part of her, really making a meal out of it.

"Cute, right?" she says. She pats her ass.

"Very, very cute." I pull the heavy blankets off of me, and she watches as I shimmy and climb off the bed, probably not-very-gracefully. I stand up, stretch a little, feel the stiffness fall away.

I can see my full reflection in the window. My naked body, my erection standing firm. Six-four, dark hair cut short, broad shoulders. Nothing at all like how my parents were, their small frames and fair hair nothing like how I was. I used to ask if I was adopted because by high-school I didn't look a thing like them, taller than my mom at least.

Her top goes straight off over her head. Her small breasts. Hard, dark nipples and tanned skin. Her blonde hair, coming a little loose from her ponytail, wilder and free. My hard-on aching for her. A slide and a snap, and she's got it her top on right.

"You look great," I tell her. "See what you do to me?" I'm pointing to my erection, which points straight to her. Her eyes gaze at it. Already, a dewdrop of pre-cum is at the tip, enticing her.

"Come here," she tells me, quietly. Wagging her finger to tell me to come closer.

In a few steps I'm next to her, towering as I lean down and start kissing her. She's warm in my arms as we begin kissing, our breathing ragged together as we go at it. Her hands are on my cock, nimble fingers pulling at it, jerking me off, already a lovely sensation forming deep in me.

I moan into her mouth. I grab her ass again, pull her closely. I'm able to take her by the butt and lift her up, placing her on the dresser carefully. If it wasn't for the yoga pants, I'd be in her already as her legs wrap around me.

My hand goes between her legs, over the tights. I can feel how warm she is, and she mumbles that she likes it into my ear. She grinds against my hand, making me push harder against her. She lifts herself slightly, and I'm able to pull her pants down around her ankles. I lean down and kiss down her neck, down her chest, down her stomach, and kneeling now, I move down to between her legs.

My tongue darts against her warmth, against her wetness. I swirl my tongue over her clit and her pussy. She holds my head against her as I go at it, kissing her thighs, darting at her mound, teasing her, before focusing my attention fully on sucking her clit. One of my hands wrapped around her leg to help keep her close to me, the other stroking my throbbing erection.

I know when she's building up to something, so I keep going. Slurping sounds on her pussy, tasting her juices and taking in the sweet aroma of her pleasure. Soon enough, her back is arching, she's squealing, coming against my mouth, the dampness pressing against my lips and chin as she wriggles against me.

After that, she's pushing me away lightly, getting me to stand in front of her as she shimmies her but closer to the edge of the dresser. She's expectant, brown eyes wanting. Her legs are open, her pussy wet and glistening, waiting for my cock.

I go in, slowly sliding myself into the warm, tight heat between her legs. I know she likes it slow, and I do just that. Her face contorts in happiness as she grinds and bounces against me. Soft little breaths of pleasure from both of us, that squeaky *Ah! Ah! Ah!* coming from her with every thrust. I can feel every inch of her, feel the wetness over my cock, in my lap. Every tendon and molecule on fire with ecstasy.

I lean in to her, kiss her shoulder, start fondling her breasts. Wrapping my arms around her as I moan into her ear. Thrusting faster now, thrusting harder. Her squeaks become more frantic, our breathing fast together. I feel her body tense up as she moans, feel her tighten around my cock, before she sighs and releases. I keep going, feel myself getting closer, ready to go.

"Where do you want it?" I ask her and she smiles, kissing my cheek, glowing warm and happy. She pushes me away, and I reluctantly stop fucking her. We make out, and I can feel how warm she is, how flushed. I move in closer, ready to put it in again, ready to come inside her.

Tara keeps me away slightly, her hand on my stomach just above my cock. It's throbbing. Slick and aching and about ready to burst. She smiles, naughty and knowing. Shaking her head to tell me *no*. She lowers herself off of the dresser, gets on her knees in front of me, and begins to suck on it, her lips and teeth rubbing against the head of my erection, already moving deep down the shaft. Her hand moves in tandem with her, and she happily hums and slurps on it Instinctively, my hand goes to her head, fingers through her hair.

I can feel myself starting to flow out, begin to feel that telltale clenching in me.

"Come in my mouth," she tells me. "I don't want any on the yoga outfit, or in my hair."

Yeah. Real sexy. There's something completely unromantic about her saying that, and it's hard to figure out why I'm distracted in the moment, on the very edge of losing interest. It doesn't bug me for long, though. The way she feels on me - the way her head goes up and down on my shaft, and the way her tongue feels as she laps me up - doesn't leave me lasting very long. My hand goes very delicately to her shoulder, a slight warning.

"It's happening," I manage to say through clenched teeth as I feel the final pressure build inside of me. I come, my toes curling against the floor as I gasp, and I feel it all rush out into her mouth. "Fuck!" I exclaim.

"Mmhh," she says as she takes it, and soon I'm finished. My vision clears a little, and I move away from her. She looks up at me, smiling. I feel a little better – being on a post-orgasmic wavelength will do that to a man - but some nagging feeling in the back of my mind won't quit as she goes to the bathroom to spit my semen in the sink.

There's that little spike of annoyance right before we finished. There's something unfortunate about how she's already rinsing out her mouth and so on, to keep things the way they are for her videos. It's funny how it now makes me feel like I have a sour taste in my mouth.

CHAPTER 2 – ANNA

IT'S HAPPENING, EVEN though I don't want to believe a second of it. I try to take in every detail. The cold, grey, rainy Sunday weather. The clean and bustling coffee shop that we're sitting in. The terrible muzak piping in through the speakers in the ceiling. The little drips of my coffee on the table next to the cardboard cup.

Tommy sits across from me in his wrinkled collared shirt, jeans, and his wire-frame glasses. He's breaking up with me. He's looking me dead in the eyes, and he's doing it fairly easily as well. Cold and calculating, which isn't how he normally acts. Condescending too, which is a habit he's tried to break before. To little success, it seems.

"My feelings for you lately, they just never seem to fit, or work out. I know deep down that there's one way I have to feel if I love you, and it just...it takes forever to get there," he tells me. It all seems like muffled noise. I know him, hell, we've been dating for almost a year-and-a-half now. We were on the cusp of moving in together. I had brief, entertaining thoughts of possible wedding bells.

"Are you serious?" I ask, and it comes out way more petulant than I wanted it to be. I've also interrupted him. I expected this sort of surprise, sprung on me like it's almost nothing, to knock the wind out of my sails. It doesn't. It's more of a slow deflation as the realization steamrolls over me.

"Of course I'm serious," he says. His calm, placating, babying voice. Yes, it annoyed me slightly before, but now it's grating. "I'm breaking up with you."

He takes a sip of his coffee, not really bothered by the whole thing or maybe trying to hide how he really feels. He takes me to my favorite breakfast place to do this? After we had spent the night together? Perfunctory, lackluster sex, to be fair. That happens sometimes! I still liked cuddling after. For the most part.

He probably just wanted one last fuck in before ditching me in front of all the Sunday morning patrons, while I sipped on my own favorite coffee and now he's gone and ruined the breakfast place I hold so dear.

"Why?" I intone. My throat feels swollen, dry. This new thing in my life hurts, and it bugs me that it's not a fully mutual ending to the relationship.

"Anna, come on, think about it. For just a second." He looks away, watches the city street and the people pass by. I want to yell at him and insult his balding head – which I know is a sore spot and something I wouldn't do normally - but I can't. Not in front of everyone.

"Is it someone else?" I ask. I know I'm better than this, but you always have to ask these things, always have to think the worst. He scoffs.

"Are you kidding me? Of course not!" he exclaims. An older gentleman at the table next to us glances over the top of his newspaper, briefly seeing what the deal is before returning to stock market news.

Well, if it's not that, then it's the only other thing, it could possibly be. It's come up before.

"It's my work," I tell him, finally dawning on me. "How much I work." For the past twenty years, I had been freelancing for various companies, helping facilitate their marketing strategies and project launches. I never stayed anywhere full time, but even with freelancing, the work carried long hours. Great pay, plus overtime. It was just one tough project to the next without too much rest.

"You're not a workaholic, or anything. But it is quite a lot," he's able to muster up. It's kind of pathetic. "I don't care about the hours, butt you're..." he pauses, looks for the right words. "You're still just a freelancer."

"So?" Defiant, my arms crossing in front of my chest. I hate my boobs, curse my curvy body, because when I do this they squeeze together always bring attention to themselves. Even though he's ending our relationship, Tommy still can't help but stare at them briefly. *Men.*

"So! You're forty-five! Time to settle down, don't you think? How many places have offered you full time work, only you turn them down?"

"This is what this about? This is crazy!"

"It's about stability. It's about maturity."

"Work isn't the only thing that makes you mature!" I say, my voice raised a little higher than I want it to be. Newspaper man gives another look. "Football with the boys all weekend long is mature? Binging TV shows instead of, I don't know, getting out and doing things?" I'm getting my hackles up, trying to punch down at his habits. Which, for all I know, are normal as anything.

"Life doesn't have to be about doing things all the time," he retorts, trying to be a calm side to thing as my energy surges. "It's just not working out. I met this beautiful, successful-"

"Oh, please," I sarcastically spit out.

"-woman and you're not doing anything about your life. Nothing about your future. It's easy to coast on just working. Going from company to company isn't exactly prudent, or thinking of a future. No retirement fund. No future." He ignores the money I make, the time off I get between jobs that's lets us hang out, a savings account as voluptuous as I am.

He just wants something I'm not. Routine. I worked incredibly hard to get where I am, find amazing employers, have a resumé that anyone would be jealous of.

"If you want to stay together, I need someone who thinks of their future, who thinks of who they want to be," he says. A rehearsed final word on things if I've ever heard one.

"Finding a permanent job would be coasting." I take a deep breath, pause myself. I'm tired of this, exhaustion centered like a weight in my brain. "Guess what? I *am* who I want to be. If you don't want to be a part of it, so be it." This causes him to look away, to know that he's lost whatever argument he had built in his head. Some pride swells up in me. "Break up with me. It is what it is. Go be whatever. Find some boring loser to spend the rest of your days with. I don't need you to be an anchor around me."

I lean back in my chair, my arms still crossed, and turn away to look out the window. The old "petulant child look". He audibly sighs.

"Some of my stuff is still at your place," he says. I refuse to even so much as glance in his direction.

"Then go get it. I don't want to see you anymore. Leave the keys in the mailbox." I keep looking out the window, the seconds dragging on longer than they ever should. Eventually, he gets up to leave. As he gets up, his chair squeaks against the floor, long and dragged out and one last stab of the knife against me. One last irritant.

The bells that hang by the coffee shop door chime as he leaves. Tommy becomes a shadow and shape walking down the busy street and away from me.

"Dammit," I mutter to myself. I feel angry, sad, annoyed. *What great timing, Tommy!* I have to start my new job tomorrow too. All these young I.T. kids will be looking for marketing help from me, the old industry pro, and now I have this new life weighing on my shoulders? *Great.*

CHAPTER 3 – MARK

CLASSSEVEN, THE COMPANY I founded with two of my friends just over two years ago, has an office that's a lot like my condo. Ceiling-to-floor glass windows, sharp edges, a modern coolness to it that borders on parody sometimes. We're still moderately small for an up-and-coming company, but these fancy offices still wouldn't have been my first choice.

I wanted something else. More warmth and some privacy. Something a little more old school, away from every other tech company in the city and not smack dab in some skyscraper. One of our first investors wanted us to come here, and since he was fronting the money for it, I couldn't tell him no. I'm probably the only one who minds.

I arrived at the office promptly at seven, an absolutely unholy hour, letting Tara sleep in and snore quietly between her ugly dark-blue mouthguard pieces. Our clients have a medical app they'd like us to make, and the next few months would be getting the tests and the coding up to snuff, the product marketed, and finally released. Today's the first busy day of many.

Already the office is a hive of activity, filled with the sounds of phones ringing. Copiers rumble, printers whizz. Fresh pots of coffee are brewed with regularity. At least it's a brighter, sunnier day than yesterday, the early sun shining nicely through those damn gaudy, damn large windows.

An early morning already dealing with a very tense call from the clients, who are an international firm relying heavily on us to see their business take off in the next couple of months. It leaves me in a huff, and I head out down the hall to what everyone calls "the bullpen". It's the open-office area with some desk, cubicles, and more than a few ways to wind down and be distracted.

The investors insisted we get a foosball table for everyone. We used to have frisbees, but too many people were getting hit in the face and I put a stop to that. Now it's mostly just a chatting area, a way for everyone to share meals, for the ten or eleven other co-workers to chat and work things outs.

And yes, play a few games of foosball for stress relief.

This is where Cody and Sean, the two guys I had founded the company with, sat. They still seemed stuck in their college days. Casual dress, longer hair, happy to play online poker, go to basketball games, and rub elbows with everyone in our bullpen. I can see why. I thought they were cheering on my skill as they made me head of ClassSeven. I thought they were recognizing all the effort and toil I gave to starting the company by gifting me my own corner office, and bestowing the illustrious but still-vague title of Founder upon me. That was only part of it. The other part was the lack of responsibility. They could code and be left alone for hours. I get the early morning chit-chats with people applying pressure, already trying to micro-manage.

"Did it go well?" Cody asks me as he tosses a small squishy football to Sean, who catches it easily. "You look like you've already gone twelve rounds."

"Could be better," I say, leaning against the cubicle wall and sighing. The squishy football is tossed to me. "Could be worse."

"Speaking of could be worse," Sean says, "I saw your girlfriend's latest try-on video. Very nice!" Cody is rolling his eyes.

"Dude, lay off," he tells him.

"No way!" he replies, his voice high pitched and sarcastic. "Our buddy is dating a celebrity!"

"You knew her before she was famous," I say. "Oof, that is weird to say out loud."

"She never made workout routine videos that focused on her ass before she was famous, hence our shared interest in the things she does," Sean tells me. I throw the football back to him, hard enough that he has to react quickly before it pings off his head.

Caitlin, our pixie-sized and endlessly exuberant receptionist, comes in with bright smiles for all of us, her petite frame bobbing in excitement. How she got so energetic is anyone's guess. Cody thinks it's cocaine but there's no definitive proof.

"Hey guys!" she says. We wave to her, perfunctory. We're all groggy still. Not on her level of excitement at all. "Anna is here! Anna McLean? Want to welcome her?"

Oh yeah, the new employee. Highly recommended. Older than all of us, but at the top of her game and willing to work with an upstart company like ClassSeven. When her resumé crossed my desk, every reference I consulted said the same thing, and said it emphatically: *Just hire her, pay her whatever, and it'll be smooth sailing until this is over.*

So now she's freelancing for us. No questions asked. Easy-breezy.

She comes from the outer hallway, the one near our entrance, into the bullpen wearing a nice fitting pantsuit, and I immediately look away, slightly embarrassed. Long, raven hair, pale skin, bright green eyes. Tall, with a total hourglass figure and voluptuous, dangerous curves. When you've worked in an office long enough, you figure out when people are dressing to hide things, and I could tell immediately that she was downplaying whatever was underneath her clothes.

I didn't know what I was expecting. Certainly not this. Call it presumptuous, but I didn't expect someone older than everyone else in the office, and someone who seemed to work non-stop, to be such a...such a...

Such a knockout.

Seriously. A knock-down, dragged-across-concrete, straight-up pinup model figure in our office. If I think about Tara – petite, angular, almost a straight line up-and-down – then Anna is the total and complete opposite of her.

Still, I push these very male, very chauvinistic thoughts deep down inside of me, and smile at her, making my way over to her for introductions. I put on the professional side of myself, acting out things the way I would do if a client or anyone else important was visiting. The closer I move to her, the more I'm taken with her, though, and I have to double down on stopping any forward momentum to any vulgar thoughts I might be thinking. Despite that honey-vanilla scent in my nose.

"Anna! Nice to finally meet you!" I tell her, my hand reaching out for a handshake. "Mark Hannon."

We shake hands, which shakes her a little, distracting me with the jiggle I can see beneath the pantsuit. I immediately go back to looking to her eyes. There's a flicker there, and I can tell she's caught me right in the act, but is choosing to ignore it. Probably used to it. I hope.

"Anna McLean. Nice to meet you too." A mature, almost smoky voice. Another opposite of Tara's squeaks and girlish mannerisms. Something more refined. She goes around to Sean, Cody, and the other employees. Shaking hands, making introductions becoming part of the team. The phone at reception rings and Caitlin runs to get it, bolting away like lightning.

"Finally nice to meet the man who hired me!" she says, once she's circled back to where I am. It's a little forced, and it's probably not so nice for her to resume talking to me after my bad first impression. I can see Caitlin bobbing around behind her, rocketing from the hallway.

"The client's on line one," she says to me. "Needs to clarify just one point." I can feel my face fall.

"Sorry about this, I have to take it," I tell Anna. "Can we talk about things in twenty minutes or so?"

"Absolutely," she replies, nodding vigorously. I step away from everything, and head down the hall back to my isolated office to take the call. I can hear Caitlin's voice start to point Anna to where the coffee maker is, where the cereal bar is, all about the epic matches that have ever occurred at the foosball table.

I'VE FINISHED THE CALL and I'm sitting at my desk, more than slightly annoyed at things and how they're already going with these clients. I can't let it get me down, can't let it sour my mood too much, because Anna knocks at the door and I have to put on a positive face so she doesn't run screaming for easier work on her first day.

I can see her framed in the doorway, see how she's taller than most women I know. See that figure of hers. I never had much interest in curvy women – just look at Tara – but something about Anna entrances me, leaves me stupefied. Once again, I slam my feelings down deep within me. I will myself an image of any dirty thoughts I have getting crumpled into a ball and dunked into a recycling container.

"Come in!" I call out. She enters, and I motion to the seat across the desk from me. I see she's holding a coffee cup from Kirsch's, one that's sharing her hand with a blue file folder. I wave at it. "Kirsch's! I love that place." She smiles as she sits down, but there's something behind it. Sadness?

"Yeah, best coffee in the city."

"I don't get the coffee there normally. More of a scone man myself," I reply. Feeling a little foolish. Immature in front of the older woman.

"They're great too!" she replies. The sadness in her smile is gone, just a fleeting thing. Probably just imagining things. A moment of silence as she takes a sip from the cup. Red lipstick sticks to the lid, leaving a small stain.

"So, I just wanted to say thanks again for coming on with us," I tell her. "We're really in need of some help here. In fact, you're probably the first new person we've hired in a year." She nods, listening. "We're developing this medical app, but because of the push to get it out from the client, we'll be starting the marketing rollout early, when we don't have all the proper resources all lined up and ready to go. That's where you come in."

"Absolutely," she replies. "Here." She passes me the folder across the desk and I open it. A multi-point plan of what she wants to do with things. "I made that. It's fairly standard, but I adjusted it for what ClassSeven needs and what I knew about the project."

I flip through the pages, hardly hiding my surprise.

"They said you were good, but this is something else. Double good," I say. Looking up at her, she has a prideful smile, a glimmer across her features. "You were strongly recommended by Connor Mitchell, and I can see now why that's the case."

"Oh my gosh!" she exclaims. "I love Connor. How's he doing?"

"A lot better now that you helped him market that toaster of his." We both laugh. Her's is a stormy one, from deep in her chest. I have her ample resumé with me on the desk, and start glancing through it. "You also helped him with his company's website and the total overhaul? Jee-zus. That's a really strong web presence he's got too."

She smiles at me, still glimmering, still a little playful.

"Didn't realize I still had to interview for the position," she says.

"No-no-no-no," I start, already on the defensive. "I was just trying to make conversation, just-uh-"

"I was just joking," she says. And all the pressure is off my shoulders. "You young guys, always so flummoxed." I chuckle, and nod in agreement.

"It's just...yeah. I knew Connor back in high-school. His word is bond. At least I think so. If he's trusted you with all this, then, yeah. I'm on pins and needles for what you can provide." I realize she's blushing a little, the color filling out her neck and what I can see of her chest. I exhale sharply, my own private *wowzers* at how disarmingly attractive she is.

"So, what's your story?" she asks, interrupting me before I can lamely move on to more things. She catches herself. "I mean, the story of ClassSeven."

"Well, Cody and Sean out there, I'm sure you've quickly gotten to know them-"

"They're quite something. They were setting up a bet for tonight's hockey game." I roll my eyes at that.

"Yeah, don't I know it. We went to university together and rented an apartment together. We had this idea for a video app and we sold it and it did really well."

"I use it," she says.

"Well, I thank you for your service," I say, a slight chuckle and a jokey nod in her direction. "It's what got us in the door, and now, this is what we do." I don't tell her that I'm still unsure as to the meaning of *what we do* and other small ClassSeven grievances I keep stored away.

"I mean, I don't use the app very often," she says. A bright wide, playful grin goes across her face. Holy moly, that smile has probably decimated a million guys. I can feel my face grow hot. *C'mon Mark, pull your head out of your ass.*

"Fair enough!" I say. "After that, we acquired angel investors and other venture capitalists became interested. Some friends and family threw money our way for freelance work as school ended too. Now we've been fully freelancing ourselves over the past couple of years or so."

"Young boys with their young companies," she says.

"That's twice you've mentioned age now," I say. "Is there a problem?" I really hope my voice came out okay. I wasn't being rude or derisive or anything. Just curious.

"Age isn't a problem. I've just been working for a lot of companies and all the newer ones are fresher with a younger workforce. Seems to get younger every five years or so."

"Oh! I guess I never thought about it that way." It takes me a moment to process it, but it's probably true, especially for someone who's like her, who's been in the trenches for so long. "Unfortunately things aren't always easy for us young boys trying to make it out there in the world, and that's where you're coming in. You're our first in-house freelancer, ever. We needed someone with experience, because this might kill us if we don't do well." I motion to all the papers around me.

"I appreciate it."

A strange silence falls over us. She's looking out the window, over towards the river. I can't help but trace the lines of her shoulders, up her neck, her jawline. Up to her green eyes. My throat's gone dry again and I cough a bit.

"Okay, well, uh, I guess we better get you-" I start, but my damn desk phone rings, shrill and terrible. "I guess, go see Caitlin and get setup further if you need to. Computer and security stuff. Then it's off to the races."

She gets up and leans over my desk, shaking hands again as the phone rings. As she leans I stand up - *I have no idea why!* - and now we're standing almost eye-to-eye.

"Thanks again for taking me on," she tells me. The phone rings again. "Won't let you down!"

Then she's gone, and I'm left watching her go.

CHAPTER 4 – ANNA

USUALLY, THESE YOUNGER tech guys are all sunken chests, never hiding their weaknesses. Skinny, super-pale boys with unkempt hair, twig-legs, and hoodies they've worn for four days straight. Mark was the opposite of that. Oaken, sturdy, big. Not imposing, but clearly filled out. I could tell that he worked out, took care of himself. On top of that, his eyes were a piercing blue that were completely embarrassing to maintain any gaze with.

Yeah, I was still smarting from my breakup with Tommy, so it was a weird but nice enough diversion to be so immediately smitten with this new guy. Mark seems so unassuming he probably didn't understand how attractive he actually was. Which of course, *makes him more attractive.*

As I settled in to ClassSeven, and the days passed, I began to learn a lot more about Mark Harron and the other workers at his company. Mark himself slowly but surely became a little bit of an embarrassing fixation, almost as if I had jumped headfirst into some sort of schoolgirl crush. It annoyed me to no end to be acting so girlish, but without Tommy around, I found myself filling up the time in my empty apartment more and more with "research" into Mark.

Which meant pouring over his social media, against any logic or sense.

It's easy enough. Cody and Sean very, very, quickly and very, very giddily point out his famous girlfriend, although I guess the term "famous" is relative, because I had never heard of her. Some girl named

Tara who spent a lot of time on various photo and video sites. Modelling, endless selfies, streaming video games, or doing makeup tutorials. These videos got hundreds of thousands of views, and she was constantly rattling off an event she'd be appearing at, or the company that sponsored her video.

I didn't really get the appeal at first – why is Mark into *her* of all people? - but I realized early on that she bent over a lot in her yoga videos, and bared a lot of skin during her streams. She seemed friendly enough, and mentioned her "hot, great boyfriend" and their adventures in the hundreds of vlogs she made. Sexy for those who wanted to watch her giggle in tight pants, aspirational for those looking for something else. A formula that works.

The weird thing is that, while Tara always seemed to talk about him, Mark rarely, if ever, showed up in one of her videos. I feel more than a little pathetic for going through each one of her things, but there was a giddy, stunned feeling of stumbling over an appearance by him. In one of the videos – titled, embarrassingly enough, *My BF Tries My Macaroni! Funny Ending!* - Mark's completely adorable, his confusion at the proceedings plain as day. His hand going through his hair and an embarrassed half-smile unable to move from his face. Very cute. I am mad that it makes my heart flutter.

It's Tommy, I keep telling myself. With him gone, and not returning my texts in regards to a couple of sweaters he left in the laundry basket at my place, I'm just using it as a coping mechanism, during this weird transition to new work and the new single life. Just that fresh, stabbing melancholy.

One of Tara's profiles mentions "babygirl to @markhar" and when I click the link, a private page shows up. I could click to ask him for access, but I daren't. My finger waffles over the button for a few moments before I click my phone off and wonder what the hell I'm doing with myself. This happens maybe once every week or so as I continue my work at ClassSeven.

I like the work, but I don't like the clients. In fact, I can barely tolerate them. They condescend much like how Tommy did in his worst moments. They're the older businessmen, older than me even, farming their stuff out to this young unproven crew. I understand on some level being protective of what they want built, but it's aggravating at times, and the hours went on and on.

Not that I minded too much. It took my brain off Tommy, kept me from randomly internet stalking Mark because I was stuck with him at the office. Caitlin, Sean, and Cody are a fun little gang, very clearly close and comfortable with each other. A once in a lifetime group I'm able to see work some wonders as they try to wrap up this app. Just watching them all makes me some silent observer, happy to be on the outside.

It's obvious to anyone with any sense that Caitlin likes Cody, but alas, he's far too oblivious. It's heartbreaking to see her stealing glances or seeing if he liked a joke she tells. Maybe Cody isn't in to girls. He and Sean seem attached at the hip, always betting on some random game or making plans or coming up with some kind of miniature competition. The bets are always low – twenty dollars max – and never seem to be done in dour spirits.

One day, when the network was down and the I.T. team scrambled to find a solution, Sean and Cody set up an obstacle course. Some rube-goldberg-type-thing that had them bouncing a wad of paper off tilted garbage cans, backs of chairs, and wired hoops they had set up. The winner had to buy a round of beer, time and date to be determined, for the whole office.

Everyone was shrieking with laughter as they tried to do different trick shots to no avail. It was during this, that my eyes glanced over to Mark, to really take him in. He had visited the gym earlier, coming back to a raucous office freshly showered. He looked fresh and clean, his hair still wet. It also opened up another thing about him that I hadn't realized.

He rarely-to-ever smiles. He's not cold, doesn't seem sad, but he's just...reserved, is the best way to put it. Prone to, even when hanging out in their Bullpen in the thick of it all with Sean and Cody, happily being on the sidelines of the conversation. It was a mystery. Didn't these young tech guys all want to be the face of their company? When he does laugh or smile, it's usually Sean or Cody that can pull it out of him.

"Long time friends," he explains one day when we happen to be together at the communal coffeemaker. I can hear the both of them cheering over a basketball game on the small flat screen television stuck to an out-of-the-way wall. "They helped me start this company, helped keep the lights on. Just...dependable," he says with a shrug, right when they cheer loudly at some point. Very clearly not working. "Despite what you see," he adds on. An ironic smirk, but that's it. He finishes pouring a mug and heads back to his office.

I watch him go, maybe looking at his butt longer than I should have. I don't feel as guilty as I could, because I also catch him looking at me more than I remembered to count. Usually peeking at my chest, or sometimes I catch him looking away when I turn to face him about something. Normally that sort of thing would annoy me, but I'm a little more ambivalent with him.

Another thing I quickly learn is that for a tech company, they seem to work harder and smarter than a lot of others I've dealt with. Yes, it's true that these guys will code and hustle and do the whole thing when the screws are applied. There has been nightmare crunch time before that I've been part of. ClassSeven never seems to procrastinate, rarely complains, and they really put in their all. Caitlin even as the receptionist with no real stake in how things go, and is free to leave right at five, stays later than she needs to, mainly to help or to set things up for the next day.

"Maybe I just like these guys," she tells me one day when I bring it up. She's looking at Cody when she says it, so that probably has more to do with it than she's willing to admit.

Things pass in a haze, but the one thing that pierces more and more distinct out of the fog of endless work is Mark. The heart skip when I see him first thing in the morning. The way I become so hyper-aware when we're close together. Tommy sliding into obsolescence, more an annoying splinter that flares occasionally rather than the fog of dread that clouded me when I started working with ClassSeven.

More often than not, on particularly hot and sticky nights where I may have thought a little too hard about Mark while alone in my bed, I find myself repeating the mantra over and over again. *He's at least twenty years younger than me. He's at least twenty years younger than me. He's at least twenty years younger than me.* Which isn't a bad thing, necessarily. It's just different. I've never pursued a younger guy before. Hell, I'm not even pursuing. I don't know how to act. He has a girlfriend. He just wants me to work here and be done with it. All I'm doing is...what exactly? Just satisfying my own interests?

CHAPTER 5 – MARK

WORK GOES ON AS IT'S supposed to. Anna proves herself time and time again. I thought the clients would throw her for a loop with their countless demands and endless micromanaging but she handles them deftly, with a sensibility that borders somewhat on severe. It's fantastic. During conference calls, I just watch her, her body language, the way she takes charge of the situation.

It's *not* a good fixation to have. Sometimes I come home to Tara – bouncing and squealing and ready to tell me about her day, ready to have fun – and there's this terrible guilt because I've been spending my time enraptured by a woman I'm working with. The workdays are long too, so having these weird, uncertain, secret, conflicting feelings brewing in me for an older woman I spend more time with than my actual girlfriend is not good.

"We should go somewhere sometime," Tara says one night, both of us lying in a post-coital glow as city lights shimmered outside. She sings a little vacation song, her head on my chest with my arm wrapped around her shoulders. My mind had drifted lazily and I'm only half-paying attention. Just wondering what Anna was up to. If she was the same way right now, leaning against some lover, and what that guy's deal was. Wondering what she would look like in Tara's position, her breasts pressed against me. Her nice round ass in my face.

My cock starts to rise again, much to Tara's happiness, and my own consternation.

"A vacation sounds good," I tell her. "Where would you like to go?" She rattles off some places other video models are going. Hotels with infinity pools. Sunsets and beaches. I'm thinking more about what ClassSeven will do after we're done with this client.

There are seeds of my own app starting to germinate in my mind. Something very early, and a risky possibility. Something I can throw to Sean and Cody at some point to see what they think. Hell, maybe Anna would be interested in it. It isn't freelance for a client. It would be our own little thing to create. Our own success or failure. ClassSeven takes precedence over a vacation, and if Anna were to stay on, we'd need to find more work to keep her employed. She's been invaluable, and deep down, I know I would miss her. Again, the guilt rises in my throat, just like bile.

Days continue, blending more and more into weeks. The dreaded "working-occasional-Saturdays" begins to be a reality. Crunch work where Caitlin happily gets on the phone and orders dinner for the whole office. Sean and Cody begin using energy drinks way more than I want them to. Even Anna, so well put together, is letting her hair just hang free some days, showing up in jeans. It's a pressure cooker ready to explode.

I go with the only idea that seems remotely viable. I decide that ClassSeven is going to have a party thrown in it's honor. It's been nothing but hard work for just a little too long. I know a work party is always the go-to solution for a difficult time for unimaginative business owners, but I'm too busy for complicated.

IT'S COMING UP ON FOUR-thirty on a Friday when I tell everyone that I'll be back shortly. The expectation is that everyone will be working late, and that I'm probably just making a snack run or something. When I return to the office, it's with Tara, who met me at the liquor store. We're both carrying enough alcohol – beer, vodka, rum – to drown an army. She's not impressed at having to carry a bunch of heavy boxes but I relish getting my muscles moving away from my desk. As I come in, it's to cheers, and I manage a half-grin under the weight of all the fluids as I put some of the boxes on the nearest desk.

"Everyone! Mandatory party time! No work allowed!" I call out. This is the most exuberant I've been, in what feels like forever. It's been a long week, and I'm tired. Caitlin starts grabbing red plastic cups from a cupboard in the office kitchenette.

I'm not really one for making speeches, but everyone is starting to gather round in a small semi-circle, and Tara is beaming expectantly as she hands me a cup of beer.

"Thank you," I say, raising the cup in toast and looking at all of them one-by-one. Tiny Caitlin at the front, with Cody pretending to play bongos on her shoulders. Sean grinning wide next to them. Every other worker, the dark circles under their eyes, but still a bit of a glimmer in there. Thank goodness. "It's been insanely hard work, and I really appreciate the long hours and dedication." Looking through them all, I find Anna. Green pools staring back at me, inscrutable, wonderful sexy. She's smiling, a can of beer in her hand.

I realize I'm staring, and I cough a little, snap out of it, and it doesn't look like anyone noticed anything was up.

"Anyways, enjoy tonight. No work allowed. Do not come in this weekend. Just drinking. *Only drinking.*" I pretend to make it a threat, and people laugh. The party starts as a loud "cheers!" breaks out.

"Can you throw on some music?" I ask Tara. "Just hook the TV up to your phone, and go nuts." She smiles and pecks my cheek, walking off to play something party-ready.

"Well this is new," Anna says, walking up to me. My heart jumps a little. I briefly wonder if I there are any websites I can look up that tell you how to get over a crush immediately, because it is what it is. My eyes darting to her chest and back up to her eyes like such a typical man.

She looks good, a little more relaxed in some pants and a sweater-shirt combo.

"You mean the party thing?" I ask.

"Yeah. ClassSeven is always so serious. I've never seen so many young people just wanting to work." She makes a goofy, faux-serious face, an exaggerated frown that is about forty levels of adorable and heart-wrenching.

"I'm full of surprises."

"I wonder what others you have planned," she says, a playful little smirk on her face. I can feel my chest and neck start to flush, go red.

"Don't know yet," is all I can say into my cup of beer. I guess I didn't realize that the music had kicked off already – too focused on Anna, damn! - and Tara bounds back, her favorite vodka-cranberry in her hand.

"Tara!" I say, probably too loudly. "This is the freelancer I told you about." I motion to Anna, and they shake hands. "Anna McLean."

"Oh my god!" Tara says. "Nice to finally meet you!" She's got a little bit of the squeaky voice. Normally it's so controlled in her videos, but she's excited and ready to party. "I've heard so much about you."

Which isn't true at all. Sure, I've mentioned Anna to Tara a couple of times - *Hey! We have a new hire! She's an older woman!* - but I really, *really* don't talk about her much. Considering certain ways I'm feeling, something in me decided to put the kibosh on ever sharing too much about her.

I wish I could say it was easy to play the double life. A lot of guys my age, and in this industry, lead some sort of double life, dating multiple girls. But I can't do it. Too wracked with guilt when I'm only *thinking* about Anna. I can barely think about making a move on her.

Watching her when she stretches up to get something from a high-up shelf, taking in every little move and agape at the way her body articulates, getting well and thoroughly excited by catching a little bit of skin at her hips and tummy as her shirt raises a bit, makes me feel guilty and horny in equal measure. What chance do I have if we were to ever do anything?

I try to push these thoughts out of my head. Anna definitely isn't interested in me. Flirty, maybe, but that's probably just a little stress valve for the pressures of working? I have a girlfriend. I'm some young *boy* in her eyes. Things are busy. I really, really, *really* have to try and stop obsessing over all of this, so I try to shove it out of my head. I decide to party. Really throwing my beer down my throat, and going to mingle.

Things eventually smooth out, and people loosen up as the party goes on. Thank the heavens. Dance music plays from Tara's phone. People are laughing, showing each other funny videos. Talking about anything other than work. It's all hustle and bustle. Sean and Cody have set up a new ball-throwing-obstacle-course-thing and Anna is trying to get a ping pong ball to bounce off several cabinets and into a coffee cup at the end of the hall.

Tipsy Tara is very flirty with me right now, and I'm grinning sheepishly as she clings to me, watching the game proceed.

"Mmm, I should show up at your office more often," she says, her hand on my butt, her mouth whispering close to my ear. "You could take me up against the photocopier." I'm trying to act casual, trying to fight the feeling that I could do that exactly, right now. I have no idea who would be around, who might see it. It would be absolutely mortifying if Caitlin – or worse, Anna – saw us doing anything.

"That would be nice," I say, overly casual. Forced ambivalence. *Keep calm and carry on*, as they say.

"Think about it." Her hands get dangerously close to my cock, playfully pattering over my belt. "You're sitting at your desk on a conference call with those mean, *old* clients of yours, and I'm on my knees in front of you. Sucking your cock while you work. Under your desk so no one knows."

I kiss her on the lips, softly, mainly to get her to stop talking about this stuff in front of other people. I'm becoming quite the jerk. I doubt anyone can hear her, and to those in the room, we just look like a couple being flirty with one another. She's not being loud or boorish or whatever you would call it. It's just a little embarrassing. I move away from her and mingle some more. A defensive maneuver.

Soon, though, it's that time where everything is winding down. Some people have left already. An air of exhaustion is settling in.

"Listen, I have to get back," Tara says, unplugging her phone from the system and killing the music. "Early morning tomorrow to talk with the lingerie people. You coming?" I know that, considering how she was talking earlier, that she wants to fool around back at the condo, but there's a pit in my stomach that I can't seem to get rid of. A malaise or depression that comes from drinking. I shake my head, already reality settling in as the party unwinds.

"I've just got a few things to finish up first."

"What happened to no one working for the rest of the weekend?"

"I meant that about everyone else. I've got a couple of things still hanging over me. Probably shouldn't have had the party in the first place."

She kisses me, her hand on my cheek. Supportive.

"Don't say that, baby. Everyone had fun." She picks up her bag and starts saying her goodbyes to Cody and the rest in the office. I sip at my booze, some rum and cola concoction that isn't very good, but Tara made it for me so it's what I've got to deal with.

Yeah, I'm a little buzzed, but it's tempered with loneliness. A slight annoyance at some vague thing. I do what I can and shove them away.

Sean and Cody are considering keeping the party going somewhere else. Caitlin and Anna stand around them, halfheartedly listening. I slide in next to Anna. Playing with fire by standing a little too close to her. She doesn't move, which isn't nothing. Shit, I'm being bad. Overanalyzing every little atom of whatever-this-is.

"Everywhere's going to be busy as hell, it's late Friday night already," Cody argues.

"Doesn't matter, man. Let's figure this out!" Sean argues back before looking at me. "Are you coming out with us?" I shake my head.

"Nah, I'm good. Tired."

"I saw Tara clinging to you," Cailtin says with a lascivious smile. "Maybe you've got other plans." Her voice drips with innuendo and I sigh.

"Nothing like that," I say, probably not very convincingly.

"Maybe cool it on the girlfriend talk," Anna interjects.

"Sure thing, *mom*," Sean says with a sneaky little grin. Anna isn't frazzled at all, though.

"I don't think it's any of our business what they do, and hey, we're still at work. Technically." She sips from her cup, a little slurp.

"Tara talks about it though, on her video page!" Caitlin exclaims, just remembering something, her eyes lit up. "There was something about it, like a little while ago. Dang, can't remember when! It's gonna kill me!" She goes to her phone, and I see the video search light up.

"It's very weird," I interject. "I guess. I don't like it, but she kind of *has* to talk about it. Makes her more open to her fans."

"Never thought about it that way," Sean says, semi-drunkenly pondering the vast wonders of social media.

"I grew up without everyone online," says Anna. "Yeah, yeah, I'm old, *I know*." It's a dismissive tone, a joking one that's very clear that she doesn't really care. "I guess you never really had this, but there was a time where you would keep secrets. Being online was kind of scary, and sharing stuff wasn't what you really did." She shrugs. "If that's what she wants to do, it's her thing. I'm sure it's very lucrative," she says, looking at me.

"Yeah," is my only reply to that. I don't know how much money Tara makes, but it's certainly enough that she's independent.

"So she shares online. Doesn't mean we have to hear about it here." It's a nice little button on the topic.

"It must really bother you," Cody says to her. She considers it for a second and shrugs.

"I think it bothers Mark more," she ends up saying. My heart warms a touch.

"Speaking of sharing things online!" Caitlin squeals out suddenly. "Let's take a photo! Everyone smush together! Before this all gets too serious." Cody and Sean hop up from their seats and stand by me as Caitlin holds up her phone and flaps her arms for everyone to get close.

Anna's right next to me. No space. Her breast pushing against my arm until I put my hand on the small of her back. This sudden change has me spiraling a bit, excitement rattling my skull. My hand slips lower, just barely above her ass as the photo is taken, everyone smiling saying "ClassSeven!" together.

My hand lingers. No one else seems to notice, and Anna doesn't seem to mind. We lean in close when Caitlin shows us the photo. It's sweet enough. Everyone smiling, a little frazzled from beer.

"Send that to me," I say. "That's a good one." And I remove my hand, even though I really, really, *really* don't want to.

The party finally wraps up, everyone dispersing into the night. Anna heads home, seemingly in a rush after that little photo was taken. I figure I've probably screwed up somewhere. Caitlin, Sean and Cody are going to some barcade-speakeasy thing I haven't heard of. I very briefly consider joining them when they ask me, but then I remember that I have to stick around to finish a small amount of paperwork, and that Tara would chew me out for not coming home right away. I text her to let her know I'll be home after things wrap up.

Finally. Some time to myself. Wonderful silence in my empty corner office. That good feeling that everything at the end of the day is finally finishing up. This app and it's marketing will get out the door on time. People had fun at the party. It was a good idea, and deep down, I'm glad I did it.

The paperwork is easy enough to finish, and I get up to leave. I start picking things up from my desk, trying to tidy, even just a little bit, and I find the file folder that Anna had fixed up when she first started here. Her fantastic little outline of stuff, the biggest, ballsiest way to get ahead of things.

I'm still in awe, still shaking my head at how intelligent it was, and how little modification was required to implement it with ClassSeven. Anna is a lifesaver, genuinely and truly. I was worried that bringing someone outside the our usual circle would result in problems, result in a transition that would be less than fruitful. I was wrong. Already, my mind is going from making her a freelancer to a permanent part of the company. She's smart as hell. Sweet. Quick on her feet.

Sexy.

I think about her black hair, and the way my hand lingered on the small of her back. How soft her sweater felt. The warmth of her underneath of it. Her curves.

I feel that familiar stretch in my pants, feel my cock getting harder. The thoughts starting to pile up in my head, swirling. It all happens in a rush. Little glimpses of her lips, her eyes, the way her breasts look from certain angles down her blouses and sweaters. The way she chews a pen while waiting on the phone.

My cock gets even harder. I can't believe it. I start rubbing it roughly, in some futile way to stop it, to apply a sense of shame through my pants. The more I think about Anna, the more it's not enough. The itch I'm trying to scratch won't go away.

I pull the zip down from my jeans, feel my cock push through my boxers, and it's free, and out, and pointing straight over my desk. The air against it feels good and cool. I'm rigid. Rock solid and throbbing. I can see the veins, feel it aching, pulsing at every vision of Anna that flits by my eyes.

No going back now. It's an empty office. Think about Anna under me, what she would feel like against my skin. Try to picture her moaning. What kind of sound she would make if I found the spots she likes.

My hand starts vigorously pumping. I'm jerking off, harder than I have in a long time. Thinking about the things I could do to Anna. The things to do with her. All the things I want her to be in this moment. My throat is dry, my heart is pounding through my chest.

More little visions, clearer and in focus now. Her in front of me, taking it from behind. Moaning happily as I enter her, as I thrust deep into her. I picture her kneeling in front of me, my erection in her mouth, her eyes happily looking into mine from under my desk as her mouth slips down the shaft of my hard-on. Grateful and satisfied as I letting my semen spurt down her throat, slick and warm.

I keep jerking my cock, and before I know it, I'm ready to pop. One more thought of Anna, her telling me to come inside her, huskily and drawn out in my ear. I feel my insides clench. Everything gets tight, and I close my eyes. Involuntarily, I let out a sighing grunt, an "oh-god-yes!" as I feel the waves crash out of me.

Cum.

Arcs and arcs of it spurt forth from the head of my cock, splatter against the desk. I nearly collapse as I finish. I realize that I'm out of breath. My legs are shaking, that this is the most I've shot in a long time. My free hand is gripping the edge of the desk, my knuckles white. All the sound in the world makes its way back to me.

Thinking about Anna has me exhausted, drained. I fall back into my chair, spent. My hand stays on my cock, gripping it. Happy and firm, pointing to the ceiling. Tingles in my toes and at the tips of my fingers.

CHAPTER 6 – ANNA

I HAD TO COME BACK to the office, forgetting my damn house keys at my desk in a half-buzzed rush to get out and get home. Thinking about Mark's hand resting *so close* to my ass had nearly discombobulated me, had thrown me for a loop. A small warmth in my stomach that I knew would cascade further unless I acted upon it.

I wanted him, and I knew, even though the thought of it *killed* me, that it wasn't exactly appropriate to take his hand and lead him into a dark corner to tear his clothes off for some fun. So I had bailed on the party pretty quickly, intending to let off some steam as soon as my apartment door shut behind me and I was able to get my underwear off.

No such luck, however, because by the time I got to the front door, when I was incredibly ready to go at myself and have a wonderful time, I had realized my mistake and had to start the long, lonely, and thoroughly unsatisfying trek back to ClassSeven.

My original motivation for rushing home had been lost in the dread of coming back downtown to the building, irritation at myself, and general aura of exhaustion overtaking any horniness I may have felt. Seeing my keys, so unassumingly resting right where I left them, not knowing the hassle they had caused me, was the little stab of annoyance I needed to really put a pin on anything I had planned to do.

I had thought everyone had gone home, so it was strange to find a light on in Mark's corner office. Hell, the rest of the office's lights had turned off, probably due to the motion sensor. I had headed over to see what the deal was. I was literally just about to grab the handle and open the door, but movement caught my eye through the crack in the door.

It was Mark. Standing over his desk. Masturbating.

My jaw dropped and I immediately had to stifle a gasp. I turned away, if only momentarily. The image of his ecstatic face, his arm pumping, had burned into my retinas. The initial shock quickly subsided and now I was all curiosity. I was suddenly back to how I was feeling before I left the party.

Do I open the door and catch him in the act? Do I run with it? No. I possibly couldn't. I really shouldn't. Tara smiling and kissing him at the party was a jealous little memory that flashed in front of my eyes.

I couldn't help it! I watched him go at himself. His breathing, his eyes, his slightly open mouth. His cock. I could tell, even from my distant position, that it was ample. Could tell by the way he stroked it that it was diamond hard. Delicious. I wanted my put my mouth on it, to feel him throb in me. I wanted to be on that desk. His hands grabbing my hips as he fucked me into oblivion.

A tingling began to pulse in my stomach and between my legs, one that I tried – very poorly – to ignore. My hand went there, rubbing my crotch through my jeans. Warm, and I could tell I was already starting to get wet. My own breathing was begin to draw out as my heart quickened.

I could see him start to clench up, start to go at himself more furiously as his back arched. He grunted.

"Oh-god-yes!" he called out. My mouth dropped again as he came. Thick, hot ropes of his semen splattered with force against his desk. The unconscious moans he had let out, the deep, hoarse breathing. I could tell that it had been an orgasm of a lifetime.

He slumped back, fell into his chair. I could still see him gripping hard onto his erect penis, slick and runny with dribbling cum. As tasty as it looked, I suddenly worried that at any moment he would open his eyes, glance over to the door, see me watching him. I would be completely horrified at what the fallout of that would be like.

Very silently, very quickly, I got out there, making sure that my keys and purse didn't jingle or jangle, making sure the front door to the office didn't slam loudly. I practically ran out of the building.

When I got home I was flushed, flustered, hot. Out of sorts and and feeling frantic. Practically tearing at myself as my apartment door shut. Pulling all my clothes off. I flung myself on the couch, laying down on my stomach, pressing my face into my pillow as I furiously used two fingers to go in and out of me. Calling out Mark's name, practically yelling, and coming hard against myself. Rarely stopping. I was absolutely insatiable. Inexhaustibly horny.

I wanted him to come like that for me. I pictured it on my chest, covering my stomach and my breasts. I wanted it on my ass, inside of me. I didn't care. I just wanted him. I fingered myself relentlessly, pinching my hard nipples.

I thought about how sweet and subdued and nice he is at the office, that cute half smile he has, mixing in with what I had seen, the passion overtaking him in that fit of vulnerability. It was a feeling very close to love, mingling with all my lust.

Eventually, after the fifth or sixth leg-shaking orgasm, I fell asleep on my couch. I woke up to early morning light, a soaking mess between my thighs. Cool and crisp air, an early morning chill sending goosebumps over my skin. My arm terribly sore from falling asleep on it. Lying there, I realized I had it *bad* for Mark Harron. Someone nearly twenty years my junior, someone taken, someone who's essentially my boss.

Someone sweet and intelligent, with a good head on his shoulders and dedication to his friends. I could feel butterflies in my stomach, fluttering with my heart, when I thought of him. To think I had been mad at my keys for bringing me back to the office.

CHAPTER 7 – MARK

A FEW WEEKS HAD PASSED since the party. Just the thought of it, and what I had done in my office, had left me in perpetual shame. Anna didn't deserve these thoughts of mine. I had to get paper towel and clean up all the cum I had left on my desk, and it felt grim, humiliating, terrible.

Anna was a freelancer who just wanted to come in to do her job, and here I was, using the way she looked to do vulgar things to myself.

Work was tough, because just seeing her reminded me of what I had done, and that I still liked her. I loved that she was experienced, loved the way she attacked tasks and seemed energized to do the best job she could. She had strong character, and was an intensely beautiful woman to boot. I loved her curves, tried desperately not to obsess over them. She didn't deserve my fawning, didn't deserve whatever I thought about her.

It was a heavy cloud, a burden I couldn't shake. It had left me in a funk. I sure as hell couldn't tell her or apologize, or bring it up with anybody.

Tara had noticed a shift in my mood. It didn't take too much for her to see that when I wasn't at work, I mostly lay in bed, and didn't talk too much. Saw that I was non-committal to any suggestions, and didn't really want to do anything. She tried to pull it out of me.

"What's up with you?" she would try. "Why are you being so grumpy today?"

"Just work."

"Well, come on, snap out of it. The party was good. Don't let anything else ruin the things you're doing." She shifted between annoyance or concern, usually more on the annoyed side of things.

It didn't take long for me to start spending time away from the office or the condo. Even working later nights, I would duck out earlier than I should have. I'd take longer lunches. Come in at a regular time rather than early in the morning, like should have. Going for walks to clear my head, or going to the gym. Trying to pump away my stress, trying to sweat out the guilt.

I had spent last night arguing with Tara. One of those smaller spats that just really needled at me, where we both snapped at each other and went to bed with everything unresolved. Turned away from each other and cold, that space between us growing and isolating across the bed linens. I had to get out of the house this morning, had to work off my stress. I got up early, and hit the streets for what would hopefully be a very long jog.

I like jogging more than any other exercise I do. I hate the treadmill. It feels horribly boring. I lift weights at the gym in my condo building or at the place near the ClassSeven offices, and that's fine enough. When I'm running, I need the change of scenery. It gets me outside, into the sun, into the fresh air. I'm worried about how pale I might be, worried about what will happen to my eyesight or posture if I'm in an office all the time or just hunched up at home.

Today I try for a different route than my usual one. I need to think, to clear my head, to get blood pumping. There's Tara and our fight. It might just fade away, unsaid resolutions just happening because, well, we live together. There's work, the inklings of that new app starting the gears in my head. I need to figure out what to do about Anna. I can't keep her on. Can't make an offer of full-time work. Do I let her go? She's too valuable. I've gone and fucked it all up. Life got very confusing and I didn't even notice.

Things in the moment are nice, at least. Feeling the sweat on my chest, feeling my breath and blood churning. I can be happy in this jog. Maybe I just need to stop being such a grouch. Maybe stop feeling bad about what I did. People orgasm to thoughts of other people all the time. I guess. I'll apologize to Tara about how I've been acting, knowing full well that it's a band-aid that will have to be addressed at a later da-

I almost stop dead in my tracks. It's Anna, standing outside a brownstone in the near distance, trying to carry some grocery bags while fumbling with her keys outside the front door. A sea of full grocery bags surrounds her feet. I guess I know what she was doing this morning.

I could just keep running. She hasn't seen me yet, and is too busy to pay attention to some random jogger. Something inside of me makes me slow down slightly, makes me take her all in as she continues to fight with everything in her hands. She's wearing jeans and a collared, pastel-colored shirt.

For once, she's not hiding anything under business clothes, and if I thought I was appreciating her figure before, I was wrong. I'm practically salivating as my eyes go up her jeans to her ass, to the front of her, and to her frustrated face. She's not wearing a bra and the thought of that sends butterflies through my stomach.

She's a stunner, no doubt about it.

I slow down my pace, walking towards her building. I'm on the sidewalk, looking up at her as she futzes around on her stoop. Six or seven stairs up, and I could be right next to her.

"Anna!" I exclaim from behind her, and I see her jump, a little surprised. She turns quickly and looks down to me.

"Oh, Mark! Hi! You scared me there."

"Sorry about that!" I'm smiling. She looks beautiful right now. Her chest and how it looks in her shirt right now is magnetic. "Just out for a jog and saw you here."

"I can tell. You look like you're having quite the workout!" It makes me a little self-conscious. Am I sweaty, beet-red mess right now?

"Are you doing alright?" I motion to the bags. With my breath returning to normal, with seeing her, I'm aware of everything. Bugs buzzing, the nice green trees lining the street, the city having itself a sunny day out. I can see her stomach, just a touch, smooth and inviting, a little muffin-top I want in my hands.

"Yeah, yeah. Just, you know, trying to get groceries in," she tells me, pointing to the bags. A goofy smile.

"Come on, let me help you," I tell her. "It can't be easy with all this stuff everywhere."

Reason has officially left me. I was literally just thinking about how I should spend way less time with her, and now I'm offering myself up on a platter. I can't help but feel a little bit excited, the guilt and shame and drive from before deflating like a balloon. To be honest, I just want to spend some time with her. Sexy or not.

She hesitates for a moment, her eyes glancing between me and the pile of bags. Finally relenting.

"Okay, come on in." She gets the keys working in the lock as I start bounding up the steps to her. "It's a little bit of mess, just warning you."

CHAPTER 8 – ANNA

IT DOESN'T TAKE LONG for Mark to get all the bags in. Normally, on a big grocery run like this I would have had Tommy's help, but the less thought about him, the better. He's been a ghost since we broke up, anyways.

Maybe Mark being here is a sign of something. I mean, he showed up when I needed help, and he looks so fucking good right now. Tight workout shirt, black shorts. Glimmering with sweat.

I've seen his apartment - his girlfriend films practically everything there - and I know that mine must look like a wreck compared to it. Smaller, older. Antique-ish things around. For Mark, it's probably a cluttered nightmare. Some old, sad spinster's next step on the path to the retirement home. A bookshelf with only textbooks and marketing things collecting dust. A corner office with a pathetically cheap and broken chair.

He starts carefully putting the groceries on my kitchen island counter, and in no time at all, it's done.

"Here you go," he says, turning to me. "Easy breezy."

"Thank you. Super appreciated!" I realize how quiet it's gotten. How the door clicking behind us has created a vacuum.

"Nice place!" he says, looking around. I hope no pictures remain of Tommy, that his balding head is nowhere to be seen. "Is your husband in or...?" he trails off.

Interesting. And not-at-all subtle. Is he wondering if I'm alone right now? There's a tingling in my stomach, my nerves suddenly pulled too tight.

"No husband. I...uh...had a breakup recently," I tell him. He nods in understanding, that common deferred nod you make if you don't know how to react, or how the other person will react to anything you say.

"Sorry."

"Don't be. Not a divorce or anything. Just a dumb breakup with a dumb man. Pretty much right before I started working with you guys." He cringes.

"I hope it wasn't our fault," he says.

"No, no. Nothing like that. Like I said, just some dumb guy." I move closer to him. "Do you want water or anything?" I motion to the fridge on the other side of the island. What is this sudden feeling I'm having? Everything's heightened. I'm buzzing and humming like a bee.

"Please, that would be wonderful." My heart is hammering as I grab a bottle out of the fridge. "He must have been super dumb. Breaking up with someone like you."

"Thank you," I say, my back still turned to him. "That's sweet of you to say." What a line. These younger guys have no subtlety. Was he flirting with me? That's at least two little lines in a row. The husband question, the breakup comment.

There's a decision to be made. I have him all alone right now, and lord knows I want him. Would he even be interested in any of this? I mean. I'm older. I look nothing at all like Tara, the skinny video superstar. We're just work friends, if you can even say that. The memory of that beautiful cock of his covered in cum crosses my mind.

A small test. Harmless. I unbutton the top button of my shirt, knowing that I've caught him looking at my chest more than once before. I think about how hard I kept coming after I had seen him. I move in front of him, handing him the cool bottle, slick with condensation. He pops it open, swigging gratefully.

"Thank you!" he says, exhaling, relieved. He realizes how close I am to him, a tiny jolt in his face that he tries to hide. *Too bad, Mark, I saw it.* I'm close enough to see his arm muscles bend and flex in fine detail as he sips the water, brings it to his mouth. Close enough that he could easily wrap his arms around me.

There's a slash of self-consciousness in his face. I see the gears turning in his mind, his own decisions being made. Is he in to me?

"Maybe I should get going," he says. He's not moving though, still leaning against the island, leaden. His eyes very pointedly looking at where my top button used to be. When he looks back up, I hold his gaze.

There's no one around. This isn't the office. I'm not catching him in any act. I want him so bad I can already feel heat between my legs, feel a dampness begin to spread. I can smell the sweat off of him, maybe the fighting lingers of some lacquered wood, earthen deodorant.

I push my leg forward, pressing my knee against the kitchen island, blocking him from moving to his left and out the door. We're totally and completely close now. Nowhere to go. Looking up at him I see how he won't break my gaze, won't make a move. Nothing ventured, nothing gained.

"Maybe stay a bit," I tell him, a husky whisper that surprises even me. A pause, a moment in time that could be short or decades long.

He leans down and into me, his arms pulling me tight. Kissing him, fully. Deeply. I can feel his tongue against mine, feel my body fall into his slightly. I feel the weight lift from my shoulders. Warmer by the moment, a pressure between my legs. Moaning into his mouth. My hands go to his waist, to the band of his shorts. My fingers trail against his abs, feel a tuft of hair below his bellybutton.

He puts his hands on my hips momentarily, squeezing, holding on tightly, but then we stop. He looks me in the eyes, fire lighting behind the blue. His breathing already deep. It only lasts a moment. He moves his hands to my shirt, and he pulls roughly, never leaving my gaze. The fabric tears away easily, a loud rip echoing slightly, the buttons bursting loose and clattering to the floor.

Gasping, I'm unable to stop the shock of my breasts falling free in front of him takes over. Quickly enough, he's burying his face into my chest, kissing at my nipples, grabbing at my ass, pulling me into him. My stomach presses against his crotch, and I'm amazed to find him already erect, already stiff as a board.

"Oh my god," I say. I'm damp already, my nipples aching and hard as he caresses them with his mouth. He pushes me over slightly, and after a small stumble, I tip back, my body going onto the couch, my hair splaying out behind me as the cushions soften the fall. Mark is between my legs, his legs bumping against my thighs. It's slightly uncomfortable: my ass is on the arm rest, the rest of me soft of the cushions.

It doesn't bother me in the slightest.

My hands go to his shorts and pull at the band, but I can't quite get a grip on them. I realize that I want it so much, my hands are shaking. At the same time, he's unbuttoning my jeans, his hands fumbling as well. He yanks at them, pulling them down roughly until they're around my ankles.

My panties, turquoise blue with a wet dark patch already, are all that's left now that my shirt is torn around my arms and chest. I realize he's breathing deep, looking between my legs, taking me in with his eyes. I feel a little self-conscious but I'm turned on beyond belief, my insides throbbing for him.

"Fuck me," I tell him. "I want it."

He pulls his shorts down in one motion, and his cock stands strong in front of me, pointing directly at my pussy. My fingers find it, stroke it slightly. More than a handful, with a weight to it I desperately need.

He leaves my panties on, choosing to pull the fabric to the side. My slit ready for him and he slides in easily. Both of us gasp sharply as the tip of his cock goes in me. Warm and willing and just for him. He leans forward, falling close so that we're kissing. He starts thrusting.

It feels more than good. His nice, hard, young, and vital cock in me. In and out. He thrusts hard. Not quickly, but deeply. With every inch of him, I start to see stars in my eyes, pleasure starting to erase everything else around us. He kisses my neck, kisses below my ear, sending shivers up my spine. One hand on my ass to hold on as he fucks me.

"Oh yes," he stutters into my ear, and just as I'm opening my eyes, he kisses me. His tongue exploring my mouth, my hand on my cheek. He holds me close and tight by my ass, the nails digging in sharply as he caresses my face.

He's very tactile. He's holding on to me like he's drowning, but he's fucking me deeper, harder. I love it. Every thrust gets a grunt from him, timed with the wet sound coming from my cunt. I begin grinding against him and it starts to feel more excellent than before.

My own soft grunting starts as I push against him, his cock hitting spots I forgot existed. His mouth sucking and licking against mine. Shivers run through my skin as we find our rhythm. My fingernails dig into his back.

"I'm gonna come," I grunt in his ear, louder than I meant to. I can feel the pressure building. "Fuck me! Fuck me! Fuck me!" I repeat to the timing of his thrusts as I push as hard as I can against his member.

All the wires inside of me pull tight, then explode. Pulsing in my stomach and in my pussy. Wave upon wave of ecstasy. I let out a a trembling moan and I'm shivering as he keeps fucking me. My pussy is soaked, and I hear how wet I am against him.

A rush. Wavelengths of ecstatic energy slicing through every single molecule. He doesn't stop, keeps me coming, draws out my orgasm as long as he can. He knows what he's doing, already tuned in how to keep me going.

I want another one. I want him to fuck me until I pass out from exhaustion. He's breathing more ragged and jittery now. I know what's about to happen and I need it. *Need it need it need it.*

A shiver breaks through him, rattling his body as he orgasms. He arches his back, pulling away from me slightly as he pumps into me, contorted in euphoria. I feel his cum in me, more of it than I expect.

"Oh fuck yes," I say, totally reflexively as it happens. More waves of pleasure build, and I'm nearly overwhelmed by it all. I'm all tingles and pins and needles. I'm television static, blurry. My mind is cotton.

"Holy fuck," he sighs into my ear. I realize my hands are still on his back, the nails dug in deep. I move them to his hair, feeling the thick of it fall over my fingers. An even newer, happier sensation. My legs are still wrapped around him. His cock is still inside of me. An extra piece of a puzzle. It feels so good inside me, I can barely register much else. I feel complete.

He goes to move, but I hold him tighter, brace myself. We're looking eye-to-eye.

His eyes shimmer, clarified. Happy and exhausted. I feel myself mirrored in them. I feel powerful, wonderful, full of light. Nothing else matters in this moment. I need him here all day, doing these things to me.

"Stay in me. Stay in me for now. I love how you feel in me." He nods, swallowing. He kisses my cheek and lingers there. The scratch of his stubble. My hand goes to his chest, under his shirt. His heartbeat is quick, but it's slowing.

He's staying hard. I'm used to guys just kind of fading, getting limp. This is new. Exciting. Something to file away for later.

"You're body is…" he trails off, still trying to catch his breath. "It's something else." I smile, and kiss him. We shift, a little strangely, I must say, because his shorts are still around his ankles, because I'm laid out weirdly on the couch, but soon enough we're lying next to each other, close on the couch together. Face-to-face.

He's out of me now, his cock sliding out as we moved onto the couch cushions. I can feel what he left in me starting to dribble out, probably leaving a very unflattering wet spot beneath me. His head is buried in my neck, one arm wrapped around me, his other hand on my ass. He's lightly kissing my shoulder.

He's still rigid as all get out, and I stroke it with the pads of my fingers. That slick, warm, just-a-bit-sticky feeling. Thinking about it inside of me, thinking about his cum being a part of me in this moment, starts to rev my engine again. My nipples harden. I'm as insatiable as when I caught him at the office.

"Does that feel good?" I ask, playful. Naughty and having no idea where to go from here, just so long as it ends up with more of him with me. He nods, his chin butting into my shoulder. The tips of his fingers gliding over my ass, between my legs. He brushes my asshole. Then my labia. Ever-so-gently. Little bits of lightning pulse down in my stomach.

"Does that?" he asks me, whispering, even though no-one is nearby whatsoever. I nod too. His hand comes around, goes between my legs. I lift one to let him in, wrap it around his hip. I begin to feel the tingles and the heat as he finds my clit and begins to rub it.

"Oh yes," I whisper back at him, my strokes matching his touches. Desperate. Needy. "You make me so fucking horny," I breathe into him. He kisses me, a hot shock to my system as his fingers find their way in me. I can feel them curl against my front, feel them rubbing against me. His palm grazing my clit.

It's all electricity. I want to gasp, but I'm in the throes of kissing him. My hands forget about his cock and swoop around his back. Pull him tight. All I can smell is him, mixing with me, as his fingers goes up and down. I writhe against him. Giddy squirming. He's holding me close, a feeling that makes me ache. His fingers relentlessly go in and out.

"Again!" I call out. "I'm gonna fucking come again!" It's not a lie. I hear myself, hear my pussy slapping against his hand, hear the wetness. When I finally open my eyes, once the starry spots have faded to an acceptable level, he's looking into my eyes. His face red, some sweat coating his forehead. He leaves a light kiss on my lips.

"I love that," he says. "You look so good when you come." He kisses me, and bites my lip a little. A pleasant exhaustion has suddenly overcome me. My own hair wet and sticking together with sweat.

"I mean, I'm exhausted, but I'm going to need you to do that about forty or more times before I let you leave," I say.

He laughs, unguarded. Wide, shining smile, with bright eyes. Lovely in this moment. A golden halo in the dark.

His phone starts ringing. Somewhere in our little push to the couch, it must have fallen to the floor. It vibrates loudly on the wood, and scares the bejesus out of me. He goes to move away from me.

"Shit," he says, his face falling as he sees who it is. Tara, obviously. He shifts off the couch to grab it, and I take in his body. Muscled. Coiled. Thick and sturdy. Well maintained pubic hair. That wonderful, hard, glistening cock. Dark pink and ready to be used.

I move and sit on the edge of the couch, needing about a gallon of water to hydrate myself. Mark ends up standing in front of me, his hard-on still shiny from me and now level with my face. I can see the throbbing veins. I can watch it bob and move as he shifts his body.

He answers the phone, his hand patting my shoulder, and rubbing my hair. Approvingly, lovingly. I can't *just* sit and stare at his hard on, so close to me. I take it in my hand and I begin to kiss it. My tongue darting over the head, my lips kissing it softly. I don't care about Tara right now.

"Hey, yeah, sorry," he says. I can hear Tara's voice, muffled but distinct on the other end of the line. The telltale high-pitched squeak. "Yeah, no, I know. Let me explain," he continues.

She seems angry. I hold his cock in my hand, feel it's weight, feel the size of it. I keep kissing it, tasting him, tasting me. The musky smell of *us*. I can feel more of his cum sliding out between my legs, know that I'm leaving another little puddle on my couch. Just a couch of puddles.

"I bumped into someone from work," he says. Not lying. "They were carrying a couch and I'm just helping them get it up the stairs. Yeah, mmmhmm."

More of her voice, but it's still muffled. Still can't hear what she's saying. It went from shrill to start, but now it seems calmer. Placated.

"Just having a glass of water or two before heading back home. We'll re-arrange our dinnertime if it's such a big deal."

I'm still gently kissing his cock. His hand goes to my hair, runs through it, and that's all the permission I need to start sucking him. My lips and mouth sliding over him, gently. My head bobs, going up and down. He gasps sharply, and I grin. We've been very naughty. "Just stubbed my toe," he says in to the phone. "Listen, I'm heading back now, I'll see you soon, 'kay? Bye, love you."

He hangs up, and I start sucking him hard, my tongue at the base of his shaft. Bobbing my head up and down. How is still *so erect* after what we've done together? Youth.

His hand in my hair stops me and he pulls away. I can't hide the look of surprise on my face. He gets on his knees and faces me, cups my cheek. He's all serious, and I realize that here comes the talk. Of an affair, of *this is just a one time thing*, all of that. My heart starts to break a little. Naughtiness is shifting into guilt.

"I have to go," he tells me. His eyes are tender, sad, regretful. My mind is already racing and I suddenly have no idea what I want him to say at all. No idea what I want to tell him.

"Okay," is all I can muster. That look on his face, the weight of it. It makes me sad. I want that smile back on his face.

"But. I don't want to. I *have* to. And I think that we should maybe continue this conversation some other time. I don't..." He trails off, still looking at me. His bright blue eyes are searching me for something. I can feel myself blushing. I've stopped touching him.

Leaning in, he kisses me, tenderly at first. On my cheek, and then on my lips. I let him in, let the kiss go deeper. I feel him holding on to my head, his hands going through my hair. The other one on my cheek. It's his way of saying he doesn't want to part with me. He must be tasting everything, but that doesn't stop him. My hand on his chest, his heart is a machine-gun. He catches his breath, but his hand is still on my face. I lean into it, kissing his fingers. All sound gone. Everything else gone. Just the two of us as far as I'm aware.

"We'll talk. I promise. I don't want this to be the end," he tells me.

I just nod at him. Watch him get up and go.

CHAPTER 9 – MARK

I'M RUNNING. RUNNING as hard and as far as my feet will take me. My legs burn. My blood's acidic. I didn't want to leave Anna there, and that's what's making me run even harder. I need to get back to Tara. Even though I really don't want to. I barrel by people on the street, some ignoring me, others staring in confusion at the guy running as hard as he can.

What just happened?

Well, I know what happened. And it fucking rocked. Anna was gorgeous. Her breasts, with those nice pink nipples. The sound of her wet pussy as I fuc-

No, don't think about that. Think about how you're an asshole. How you've cheated on your girlfriend.

A girlfriend I don't even really like anymore. Someone I stuck with because, well, I don't know why I stuck with her. It's so easy to get comfortable. It's the same with ClassSeven and what we're doing. It's easy enough, you lose your focus, and then it becomes routine and you slip away.

Anna's something else. Not a wrench in the plans. She's a caffeine boost. The refreshment I've been wanting in the back of mind for as long as I can remember. My heart's pounding due to my run, but it's also going fast just thinking about her.

The intelligence. How she always seem to have something interesting to say, a unique viewpoint. The strength she uses to handle problems. The way she put her leg out to stop me leaving.

I have to stop running, realizing just how out of breath I am. Realizing that before I left Anna's, all I wanted to do is spend time with her. Not fucking, necessarily. Even though that's fun.

I just want to hang out, and talk to her. The last thing I ever want to do is talk to Tara about yoga clothes or branding or whatever. I want to talk to someone new, someone who feels real and would have some insight into anything. Someone I can share ideas with.

I must look ridiculous to anyone passing by. Leaning against the brick wall of a laundromat, catching my breath, already the sweat is making my shirt stick to me. Some wild-eyed lunatic.

Especially now. I'm feeling like shit, caught between two people.

I know what I have to do.

I can't keep going with Tara. My happiness bumping into Anna and helping her with the groceries, as well as my ground-shaking orgasm, outweighs anything Tara has left for me.

Am I a jerk? Am I a terrible person? Of course I am. I cheated. I did a thing I always told myself I wouldn't do. But it felt good. That's the issue. Being with Tara used to feel good, but somewhere down the line it became a lifeless, odd little albatross around my neck.

I've made my decision. I know it's just going to drag out and rip me to shreds and there's going to be collateral damage. Things that are worth it are never easy, and Anna is worth all the trouble in the world.

CHAPTER 10 – ANNA

FOR THE FIRST TIME in a long time, Mark Harron is late for work.

I don't know if I should be worried or not. The Saturday was all kinds of incredible. Still thinking about the way he looked, above me and inside of me, is enough to momentarily daze me. Now I'm feeling foolish.

Sunday came and went. I waited for a phone call, or a text, or anything, and nothing happened. I was mixed between annoyed and sad and apprehensive. As Sunday evening drew to a close, I felt an overwhelming sense of dread. I didn't know how he would react, didn't know how I should act. I've never had an office fling before! I don't even know if it's a fling or not! I have to see him tomorrow!

It didn't stop me from dressing up today. Some misguided thorn in the back of my mind, where I thought I would be sexy just for him. That maybe he would want me again. Today. That there would be some surprise. No pantsuit, no professional or sensible stuff like I normally wear.

Very carefully, in it's own ritual, I put on what I thought would be my most attention-grabbing outfit. From an admittedly-limited wardrobe.

Black stockings, black garter clips. Black panties and pushup bra. Black blazer and just-above-the-knee-length black skirt. White button-up blouse. Very secretarial of me. I feel very sexy.

Unfortunately, Mark's not here to appreciate it. I can tell that Sean and Cody – as well as half the other guys in the office – dig it though.

Caitlin raises an eyebrow, but doesn't say anything. It doesn't make me feel the same good way it would if Mark was here, checking me out. I feel silly. Sexy and silly.

It doesn't matter though. I just do my work and watch the morning clock tick by. Sean and Cody commiserate at their desks as per usual. Normally, they're all you can hear in the office, jokes and whatever else. Endless laughter. Right now, they're hushed, reticent, trying to keep a secret. It's enough that Caitlin asks them what's up.

"Did you lose another one of your bets again?" she asks Cody as she leans against their cubicle walls.

"No. It's rough," Sean says, his hand going through his hair thoughtfully. "Mark and Tara broke up." Ice and fear and confusion stab through me at once. Elation too, but it's tempered by the shock.

"Oh, jeez," Caitlin says meekly, with a very Caitlin-esque gasp thrown in for good measure too. I hold my own in, but I head over to them anyways, to see what the deal is. To give some sense of anything I might be feeling right now, with the air of someone casually interested in the office gossip.

"And," Cody continues, "She posted a video about it."

"No!" Caitlin exclaims, her hands covering her mouth.

It takes every single ounce of willpower I've ever had to not pull my phone out of my pocket and look for this video immediately. I actually don't have to, because Cody does it for me. He hits play on his own phone and angles it towards us. Sean comes around too, even though he's already seen it.

The title of the video is *We Broke Up*.

It's in their condo. Tara sits on the edge of their massive bed, blanket wrapped around her legs, as if she's cold. Her eyes are puffy and red, but somehow, the rest of her makeup is still impeccable. She's not looking at the camera, but then there's an edit – a quick cut - and she's in full video blog mode now.

"So..." she starts. "Big news, I guess."

Oh no. I realize that there's a shape next to her, a shadow. A dip in the mattress. It must be Mark.

"Today, my boyfriend broke up with me," she says, her voice thick from crying. "I'm still trying to process it, but, I'm really glad I still have my fans out there in this time."

"Yikes," Cody intones, shaking his head. He shares a look with me. *You were right about sharing too much.*

"So, Mark," Tara continues, and the camera shifts slightly. My heart leaps. There he is, just as I had guessed. He looks like he wants to be anywhere else in the world at the moment. He looks like he has to face a firing squad. "Is there anything you want to tell me before this is all over?" A long pause. He exhales through his nose. No eye contact at all. Like a guilty dog.

"No. Not really." It's all he says. The camera then cuts to Tara in the bathroom, some time later. She's wearing different clothes, and her puffy eyes are even redder.

"So, you heard it here first, straight from him," she says. "He didn't even want to talk about anything." This is kind of disgusting. She begins a long diatribe about a multitude of things, but I can't focus. There's something so weird and off-putting about airing your laundry like this, and she's doing it with gusto. Still, I can't pull away from the screen.

He broke up with her. He really did. Does that mean we-

"He's been really distant lately, working a lot, late at nights," she goes on. "You know what that's code for, right, ladies?" My heart sinks further, knowing how she's spinning the narrative.. "He was probably cheating on me! You know how it is with guys! They always want more than what you can give. And I've tried! I've really tried!" She begins choking up and sobbing at this point, but Cody yanks his phone away from us, stuffing it in his pocket. It shocks us out of our absorption.

Mark's coming in through the front door. He looks like he just got finished at the gym – a duffel bag is slung around his shoulder and he looks like he is freshly showered – and luckily, doesn't know that we were watching any breakup videos. He looks a little out of place in a very casual-for-him-at-the-office polo shirt and jeans.

"Morning everyone," he says. He sounds distracted, like his lifeforce has been sucked out of him. "Sorry I'm late." No one can say anything because he immediately makes a beeline for the hallway and heads towards his office.

"Oof-bah-boof," Sean says. "He got it bad. You can tell."

It ends up being the least productive day ever. I feel like clay, goopy and unformed. I just do the work, but I can't even tell if I'm doing it right. It's all slow as molasses. Just a strange, oppressive atmosphere.

I didn't believe that anyone could make me feel this way so soon after Tommy, but it's starting to seem more plausible with each passing hour. When I have to talk to Mark about anything – strictly work related, of course – his speech is short, clipped. Lots of "yep" and "sounds good" and "go for it", and each one feels like a knife to the chest. It's grim. I want him to feel better. My heart aches a little to see him like this. He never leaves his desk all day, except for a bathroom break.

Despite this, I end up working late anyways. Trying to be supportive, holding on to hope that Mark might pull a surprise from somewhere. The sun goes down, and things get dark, and there's nothing left for the day. I decide to head home. I'll sit on my couch and think long and hard about things. I'll put whatever feelings I have to rest.

I lean in the doorway to Mark's office, my heart absolutely hammering through my chest. So many fantasies start this way. The late-night office thing. I don't know what I'm hoping for, but it's certainly more than this – a ruffled, thoroughly depressed-looking Mark slouched in his seat.

"Well, uh, yeah," I say, meek as a mouse. "I'm heading out for the night. So. Yeah." Of course, I'm waiting for him to say something. To say anything at all. I'm practically writhing in discomfort over here.

This is my one last attempt before I really, really, really for real this time decide to give up.

He looks up to me, as if he's surprised to see me there. Those blue eyes, shocked. I see them flit to my chest, the briefest of brief moments, and there's a twinge in my heart. *Calm down Anna, there are still other people here. Be professional.*

"Yep, late night," he says. "Thank you for staying."

"No problem." The silence just kind of hangs there, awkward and terrible. This was a mistake. I didn't realize I'd be so let down that it would a one-time thing. I mean, he did say "we'll talk about it." And he broke up with his girlfriend. Maybe out of guilt.

"Well, uh..." I trail off. He's still looking at me. "I'm going to go. Grab late night dinner." I'm fully deflated now. No words to make any of us feel better. Can't believe that someone nearly half my age is letting me down like this, but that's how it is. Can't even believe I'm letting some younger guy make me feel this way. "Take care," I tell him. "See you tomorrow." I turn to leave.

"Well," he starts, and I stop, looking down the hall to the exit, too little-schoolgirl to even turn around. "If you're looking for late night dinner, there's Martino's Pizza. They do great slices."

Another pause. Nothing. Confusing. Don't really know why he'd be recommending pizza. Especially after full on silence and coldness all day long.

"Okay, maybe," I say. Still not looking at him.

"I..." he trails off again. I hear the rustling of papers, but I don't dare look towards him, don't expect anything. "I find that the pizzas there are best, like, around ten-thirty-ish. Today's Monday, right? Monday, ten-thirty, Martino's...on Boxler Avenue. I have a feeling I might be there. That's my kind of thing."

Little brat. He knows there are still other people around, some others putting work in, and he knows that there are others possibly listening, looking for a mood change.

"Sounds like a dream," I say. And walk towards the door. Guess I do have plans for tonight.

Due to the time it would take just getting to Martino's, I won't really have time to change into anything. Damn these long hours. Do I really plan on showing up there in what I was wearing to the office in the first place? I'll have to. Just completely out of place.

I get to Martino's around ten-twenty-five. It's in the opposite side of town as the office, in an area of town that seems to be newly gentrifying. Hip couples sip craft beers on patios. It's far from where Mark's condo would be.

Martino's is a little bit of dive compared to the other places surrounding it. A corner building, nestled on the ground floor of a converted house, it's practically empty. Just an old guy behind the counter, silver hair and rotund, wearing history's dirtiest apron under buzzing florescent lights. I smile in his direction and he nods, but he doesn't really pay much attention to me as he goes about making pizza. I sit down at a table that has definitely seen endless parties and slices over several decades, and I wait.

And I wait some more. Ten-forty, and he's not here. I think about texting him. I shake my head and chastise myself. I'm acting genuinely crazy. Ten minutes isn't too late, nothing to get in a tizzy about. How many times have I gone an internet date where the guy's late? Ten minutes is barely anything on the scale of it all.

By ten-fifty, I'm pissed. More at myself than anything. Of course I tricked myself into thinking it might be more than a one time thing. I try to run through what he said in my head as I grab my coat, ready to head out the door. No more looks from the guy behind the counter, expecting me to buy a slice of pizza.

But then, there he is. Mark's at the door, apologies spread out across his features. A little dumbfounded too.

"Sorry! Damn, I am *so* sorry," he says profusely. "I got held up with some client bullshit. Had to basically run here."

I nod brusquely, still trying to process things. He looks cute. A little out of sorts, and yes, sweating as if he ran here, as his hand goes through his hair. He looks at my coat in my hand, then his eyes meet mine, and they glimmer with an inner smile. He looks awed. He looks like he really, really wants me to stay.

"Mark!" the guy behind the counter yells. "I see you're making this lovely woman wait! You are a bad man!"

"Yeah, sorry about that," he says to him. One last look to me. That passing look. *Are we okay?* I smile, and put my coat back down at the table, and we both move to the counter.

I'll admit. I'm starving. Working late with no dinner, and sitting in a pizzeria smelling freshly cooked *everything* for twenty or so minutes will do that to me.

CHAPTER 11 – MARK

CRISIS AVERTED. MOMENTARILY. With a nod from Anna, I very sheepishly go to the counter. Ready for my balls to be busted.

"Sorry Sal," I tell the chef as he stares at me, incredulous from behind the counter. "You know how it is."

"That's right, big money man! Too important, it seems!" he says, making a big show in front of Anna. "Don't go losing your head, forgetting the important things in life!"

"I know, I know…"

"In my experience, no matter who you are, never leave a lady waiting," he calls out, smiling. "Thirty years ago, I had a date with the most beautiful piece of woman you could ever ask for," he starts, but then looks to Anna. "Except for you, my lovely." She giggles, and I roll my eyes. "I was five minutes late for that date and she was already gone and already with my best friend! Can you even believe that?"

"I can't," I tell him, flatly. I've heard the story before.

"So! Never, ever leave a woman waiting!"

"Good advice," Anna tells me. I turn to her and she's smiling, clearly teasing.

"Yeah, yeah. However, the best pizza in the city is worth any wait. One pepperoni slice and a water for me," I say to Sal. I'm absolutely starving as pouting in my office without lunch or dinner has left my stomach rumbling.

"And for the lady?" he asks her, as he goes to heat my own piece of heaven up.

"I'll order, but I have to know. If you're Sal, where's Martino?" she asks him. He smiles wide.

"Oh Martino's around, he's just a little shy."

"Martino is Sal's cat," I explain. "He's a fur-covered demon."

"Guard cat! An he's no demon. Just temperamental," Sal says. Anna chuckles, light, sweet. I am such a stupid schoolboy with a crush. I look away from her to stop from blushing, stop the fluttering butterflies. The day has been a wreck, with Tara and all of that, but that laugh might make it all worth it.

"Well then, Sal, same as Mark. Pepperoni slice. But give me a Sprite instead of the water."

"No problem!"

After a few silent, awkward moments of me totally avoiding Anna's eyes while waiting for our pizza, we sit at the one table by the window. A couple come in and order from Sal, a takeout request that keeps him busy. I know he's watching us from the corner of his eye, keeping supervision.

It's just another Monday in the city. Cars drive by on the street, and we can hear them through the open door. Maybe I should have picked a nicer place for us to eat.

"Sorry again about being late. And sorry for just getting pizza...maybe you were expecting, like, Cherinni's or something five-star like that." I barely know what either of us is expecting at any moment.

"Stop saying sorry," Anna says, and she takes another bite of pizza. "This is really the best pizza I've had in a long time. So I'm glad." I take my own bite, a big one, to keep my mouth shut and to distract me. "So, the client?" I nod as I finish chewing.

"Some last minute issues which could have waited until tomorrow. But you know how it is."

"I do. I think I have you beat on experience," she says with a smirk. "Twenty years of it, I think."

"Which means I *have* to ask. Why are you, you know, just freelancing? I saw your resumé. It's intimidating," I tell her, with a big silly grin. She smiles too, her eyes bright as she offers her own shrug.

"Could never find the right place, and it's always easier to get something this way. I can have connections and references and networking but I don't want to be tied down. I expect a very kind reference letter when this is all said and done."

"Ah, shit." I sigh. "I was going to offer you a permanent position at the end of the week."

She looks completely shocked, shifts in her seat a bit and looks right at me. When her legs move, they bump against mine. Our knees touch, our calves rest against each other, but we daren't move them. I blush, because she's definitely giving me a playful look right now. A small, knowing smirk across those sexy lips of hers. She knows what she's doing to me. I swallow some water - my throat is suddenly incredibly dry - and look out at the passing cars.

"A permanent position?" she finally says.

"Yeah, sorry for spoiling the surprise."

"It definitely is. A surprise, I mean. Not spoiled."

"Head Marketing Manager. We have healthcare, insurance, that kind of thing." It's her turn to look out the window, some strange, inscrutable across her face now.

"Maybe, let's not talk about that at the moment. The way things are." I know what she means, but I have no idea how to continue, or how to tell her that it's okay.

My hand goes under the table and to her leg. I give her a re-affirming squeeze on her knee, and she turns back to me, with a smile. I shift slightly, and as I do so, she takes that same hand in hers. Puts it on the table and holds on.

"I'm sure we'll talk about it at some point, but for now, I'm just going to enjoy my pizza and not think about work or dumb clients or late hours," she says. Another big bite of pizza, and I smile at her.

"No shop talk, can do," is all I say, and for real, I leave it at that.

"It must be nice, being the head of a company, though," she says. "Especially at such a young age, like yourself."

"I'm not *that* young."

"Hrmm, I don't know about that," she says. "But I don't mind it." She's being really flirty. After what had happened, I can't blame her. When things haven't been crazy, it's all I think about.

"I just sort of fell into things. And we make other people's stuff. It's not special. Yet."

"Oh please, you didn't just fall into it. Why the name? You came up with that. Cody told me."

"ClassSeven?"

"Yeah. It's a weird one." I had been hoping to avoid the whole story, but sometimes these sorts of things are inevitable. I sigh.

"In high-school, I took an afternoon coding class thing. It was in the computer lab. Normally we would have six periods – math, history, all of that – but I'd have this unofficial seventh class at the end of the day."

"Ah, okay," she says, nodding and getting it immediately. I could stop here, tell only the incomplete story. With her hand in mine, with her smile, with the way my feelings for her are percolating in my head constantly, I tell her the full tale. Something I waited for forever to tell Tara, but I can't help it with Anna. I feel like I can trust her more, to be more mature about it.

"That's how I got interested in all of...whatever. Tech, running companies, on-and-on. It was my parents' idea that I go," I say. "I was completely, totally, one-hundred-percent against it with every fiber of my being. I just wanted to play videogames after school. After school shit was for losers in my eye. But they pushed me to do it, and it ended up changing my life."

"They must be proud of you, then," she says. I shake my head slightly, and I'm not really looking at her, choosing to watch traffic go by.

"I think they were. Uh, I guess..." I try to find the right words. Delay, delay, delay. *Ugh, just spit it out.* "My parents passed away around that time. Right when I was in high-school."

"Oh no. I'm so sorry," she says. Her hand grips mine a little tighter.

"Not your fault," I say. It's the standard response. "What had happened was...I had been doing this class for a while. It always kept me at school until about dinnertime. I came home one day, and they were both, uh, just kind-of sleeping on the couch. Carbon monoxide poisoning."

"Oh no," she says, a sad sigh.

"The thing is, if I didn't have my class to go to, I would have been dead too. Slumped over my homework or a controller. I would have been home. So the name's a little bit of a tribute. They saved my life in more ways than one."

"Wow. I'm sorry. I don't know what to say."

"Don't worry about it," I say. "It happened, long before we met. Nothing to do with you-"

"Still, I'm sorry, that-"

"Now, who's the one saying they're sorry too much?" I ask, a sad smile on my face. That stops her.

"Alright, alright. Great. No problem. Fine." She is very sweet and cute when she's thrown for a loop. We less-than-subtly change the subject.

We end up talking so long about so many things, that Sal has to kick us out as the night winds up.

"I'm closing up shop!" he calls out. "You ain't gotta go home, but you can't stay here!" It's enough to get us to leave. We get up and out, heading to the side of the entrance. I don't want the night to end. It's only midnight, really. From the door of Martino's, we can hear the chairs scraping, things shutting down.

"Speaking of home," she brings up. "Are you, you know, still with Tara? Living with her, I mean." It's a loaded question. She's absolutely wondering what the deal is. I just shake my head, lean against the brick wall closest to us. The light from the pizza-place window above us bathes both of us in a florescent halo.

"Tara kicked me out. So I'm actually living here now."

"She kicked you out of your own condo?" she asks, her eyes wide. "Doesn't seem fair." I shrug.

"She'll be moving out, and then I'll sell probably sell it, or something. Not really a big fan of it to begin with. I'm living here now." I motion to Sal and Martino's.

"You're living in a pizza place?"

"Above it, actually. For now." I point to the darker windows on the second floor. "Come on, I'll show you. If you want." She nods, and I motion with my head for her to follow me.

CHAPTER 12 – ANNA

WE GO AROUND THE CORNER and he unlocks a barely-visible side door attached to the same building as Martino's. We traipse up the narrow wooden stairs to the apartment. I have flashbacks to every apartment I ever had in college. Every greasy, bad party I had ever been to when I was younger. The room above Martino's is just kind of a low-rent apartment. Something you would find a few new college students out on their own renting. Which is exactly what it is.

"This is where Sean, Cody, and I started ClassSeven," Mark tells me. I try flicking on the lights, but they don't go on. "Yeah, they don't work just yet. The power's been turned off because no one was renting it."

He walks over to a cooler that surreptitiously sits on the floor while I take stock of the place. A far fall from his condo, but it doesn't seem to super-bother him. A cot, a broken armchair, that musky dust smell. He returns with two bottles of beer, unopened, and he hands me one. In the dim light, I can't even tell what brand it is, but the satisfying *pssh* of the cap opening is enough to make me take a big sip.

"So, you're living here now?" I ask him. "Or at least, going to?" He nods, sighs, plops down in the askance armchair.

"There's no sense in me being in that ugly condo. That was Tara's idea. She can have it for now." Bringing up her name stabs me in the heart with ice a little. "Plus, her little video stunt worked as well as it could."

"What do you mean?" I feel dumb and unsure of what to do with myself. I move to the bay window that looks down on to the street below. A car drives by, and the headlights are enough to fill the apartment with light. It moves from one side of the room to the other, and fades away. Mark shrugs.

"I didn't even want to be in that dumb video in the first place but she practically forced me. Said she would make things easier for her, and that we could build a series out of it. A really in-depth look at what went down. For internet content, if you can even believe it. So I'm not going back, not really dragging out the drama. Now I'm..." He trails off, looking up at me, with a sad-but-sweet smile on his face. "I'm doing that thing where you're on a date and you talk about your ex. That's, like, a no-go," he says.

He looks sheepish and adorable in this moment, and when he gets up from the chair, I'm reminded about how masculine his frame is, how tall he can actually stand. "No use wallowing in an armchair like some loser," he mumbles. He's nervous, a little fidgety. I decide I can tease him a little.

"This is a date?" I ask, a little sarcastically. I sip my beer bottle with a big grin on my face.

"Probably not the most charming place for one, I'll admit." *Whatever.*

"Come here," I tell him, shifting my feet and beckoning him to come over. He steps next to me. I'm a tall woman, but he's just that bit taller than me, and I move in to hug him, resting my head against his shoulder and hugging him from the side. He hugs back, his hand resting on the small of my back. Like this, it's hard to remember that he's twenty years younger than me. He feels mature, like a firmly planted tree. Dependable, at least in this moment. More cars go by, more lights move and paint the walls. We both just look out the window in silence, and I try to remember every little detail. I wonder briefly what he's thinking, but it all just feels so heavy. Trying to piece things together. The future feeling foggy but oh-so-close.

"Do you want to go somewhere?" he asks. It's barely above a whisper. "Like, get a real drink, somewhere? I know a good bar nearby."

What do I really want?

"Right now, I'm good here," I tell him. He holds me tighter, and despite the air of melancholy, there's this little bright spot of happiness I feel deep inside me. He leans down slightly, and kisses the top of my head. I could get used to this. Time passes in more sips. Quiet words. My heart filling up close to bursting as he tells me little stories, makes me laugh.

"We need more beer," I exclaim as I realize my bottle is empty.

"Those were the last two in the cooler," he tells me. "But Sal has some downstairs."

"The store is shut." He pulls some keys out of his pocket, jingles them.

"It's a perk of living above the place. Let's go."

"Will Sal mind? We can't just steal his stuff."

"I'll pay him back. Easy-breezy." Well, if he insists.

We actually head out through the back of the apartment, squeezing through a small bathroom window, and then shimmying down the fire escape and into, what I assume, used to be a backyard whenever this pizza place was a house. A dumpster sits by the back fence, surrounded by concrete bric-a-brac. An orange light buzzes above us, moths and other bugs flitting around it. Unlocking the back door, we stumble in the darkened pizza place. I nearly trip over the elevated step in, but Mark's able to catch me, holding on until I get my footing.

Our only lights are the orange one from the backyard coming through a window in the backdoor, and the blue glow of a soda fridge at the front counter. It's all a little eerie. He holds on to my hand, as we carefully move through the store. I'm afraid of falling face first into a stack of pizza boxes. Afraid of making a real fool of myself.

"What about Martino?" I ask. "Satanic guard kitty?" This causes Mark to chuckle from the shadows.

"He's an asshole but he's no guard cat." A few more steps. He finds a regular fridge, and is able to open it. He grabs a few beers and it closes with a thud. He hands me one, cold in my hand.

"Kind of spooky," he says. "The haunted pizza parlor." I can hear his own bottle open, hear him swig. I do the same.

"Find the light then."

He takes my hand – not unpleasant in the least, and something I'm very much getting used to – and guides me into the kitchen prep area. I can't see it clearly but I know there are those big reflective steel kitchen counters around the perimeter. I'm able to put our beers down on them so we don't fall and spill everything all over ourselves and the floor.

He finds the light, and the florescents buzz to life. The stainless steel counters, ceramic tiles, and washing sinks all light up. All sterile. Mark's actually very close to me, reaching past me to the wall and the lightswitch. I catch him looking in my eyes, searching me. I feel that certain flush, feel heat between my legs. I know what's coming, and I know I want it. My throat dry now. I kind of wish I still held on to that beer but it's sadly out of reach at the moment.

"I actually kind of like it a little better all dark. More mysterious," I say. "Don't want people thinking it's open for business. Don't want our date interrupted by hungry people." I turn, finding the lightswitch. With a loud *ka-thunk*, everything goes dark again. Halos of the orange light bleed in from outside, the fridge light still on.

"Date, huh?" He's moved closer to me, his hands finding my hips. His torso against mine. I steady myself against the wall in front of me by the pads of my fingers. His cheek is against my cheek.

"Maybe," I whisper. I'm taken aback a touch, my pulse rising, my heart jittery. Excitement.

"Can I ask you something?" he goes. Still whispering. Breathing out, excited. There's a pause. I'm elastic with anticipation. "What you're wearing today, were you wearing it for me?" So he did notice. I nod. I wonder if he can even see me.

Then he's kissing my cheek, softly and sweetly, the stubble brushing against me. A peck near my cheekbone. Another lower by my jawline. Searching.

"Well, I like it," he says. His breath tickling the back of my neck. His hands move from my hips to the bottom of my skirt, trailing under it and up my thighs.

I know this won't be like before. Last time it was sudden. Spur of the moment. He had to get back to his girlfriend's place. Right now, he's really taking his time. In fact, I can tell that he's trembling a little bit. He's practically vibrating.

"Are you okay?" I ask. "You're shaking."

"I'm good," he says. I can feel him smiling. "Just..."

"Yeah?" There's a pause as he breathes. An aching pause where I just want to pounce on him.

"Really, really excited."

He finds the top of my stockings, and he slides his fingertips over the material, between the stocking and my thigh, bumping against the garter clips. I might start shaking too. I put my hands on the wall in front of me, just to steady myself. He's lightly kissing my neck, just below my ear.

"I like that," I tell him, and he keeps doing it.

"I like that you like it," he says. I laugh.

"You're so corny. It's sweet." His hands move up to my panties, feel the lower band and the soft satin. I'm all nerves and want. A tug of war between needing him to fuck my brains out right now or to wait for something just as good.

He pulls my panties off, sliding them past my knees to my ankles, around my feet. It's just my skirt and his pants blocking the way. I'm wet, excited. There's an unbearable heat between my legs. There's some motion behind me, and I instinctively arch my back, pushing my ass out for him. I turn my head, see him kneeling, his face pressing against me. A little jolt and more as he kisses my labia, sucks on my clit. One hand goes up my leg slowly before rubbing my cunt at the same time as his kisses and licks. He presses his lips together and buzzes on my clit, and it's more jolts of electricity over my body. I tremble and moan, push myself into him.

"Good boy," I tell him. "I like that." I'm sopping wet, and the sound of his slurping mixes with my grunts and moans and gasps. I'm hot as hell, sweating thorough my outfit. I have to unbutton my blouse just so I can breathe and be comfortable.

I hear him stand up, the sound of his jeans unzipping. I push myself to him. *Please fuck me. Please, please, please.* I can't see it, but I feel it. The sensation of the swollen member pressing against my wet hole. He takes my hands in his, keeps them pressed against the wall, and his shifts my legs with his. I'm spread out and ready to take it.

He enters, softly, unbearably slowly. *That fucker.* It starts off gently, us getting acclimated to our rhythms. I refuse to hold it in. I want him to go faster, to make me feel it as deep as I can. He seems to realize this, my lascivious sighs echoing through the dark kitchen.

Taking my hips in his hands, he starts going at me hard. The wet slapping sounds, his breathing, the smell of it, fills me up every sense I have. I find my clit with my hand and I'm rubbing in tandem as he goes in and out. Every nerve in my body is on fire. Everything I feel is going to one sensation.

"I'm gonna come!" I say in between furtive gasps as he repeatedly drives into me.

"You wanna come on me?" he asks. "I wanna feel it on my cock. Come on. Take it."

"I'm gonna come! I'm gonna come! *Ah!*" It builds harder and higher, and then unleashes a torrent. My legs buckle a little as he keeps thrusting into me. I squirm as spots and stars dance in my vision, as I call out in happy ecstasy. "Oh god! Oh god! Oh god!" I can't stop my orgasm, it becomes completely overwhelming, and I have to push away from him, my hands against his stomach. He stops, and I turn to him.

I must be reflected in his face. Beads of sweat on both our foreheads, our deep breathing. He doesn't take his eyes off mine, but he's pulling his shirt over his head, and I pull him close for a brief hug when he throws it to the floor. My fingers playing with his erection as he unbuttons his jeans. Letting them and his underwear fall to the ground. My hands all over his abs, feeling his muscles, grabbing at all the tight things around him.

We kiss, harder and sloppier and more passionate than ever. His cock pushing against me, the wet stickiness dragging across my stomach. His eyes are looking to my chest, and before I know it, he's burying himself into my cleavage and pulling at my blouse and blazer, trying to get them off.

"Please, be nicer to the buttons this time," I tell him, and he laughs. A full-throated, joyful, smiling laugh that has him leaning back. He's smiling again, and his eyes twinkle as he looks at me. My heart melts at that. A warmth fills my chest as he presses his forehead into mine.

"I promise," he says. More kissing. Softer. He carefully removes the blazer and then the blouse. I'm just in my bra now, everything else pooled at my feet. We step out of our clothes, kick them to the side, and I'm giggling as one of his socks stays stuck on his foot. It takes a few little silly soccer kicks to get it to fly off and go somewhere. Possibly into a deep fryer, who cares?

When I see him like this, there's nothing else. Even in the darkness and streetlight shadows, he's clear as day. Handsome and strong in so many ways. Vulnerable and sweet in others. My eyes start to water. I can't help it.

"Whoa, hey," he motions close to me, our foreheads again pressed together. Our hands at each other's hips. "You okay?" he asks. I nod.

"Yeah. This is just..." I search for the words, fumble towards something, anything, that would make sense.

"You want me to stop?"

"God, no. I just..." I trail off. "This is, like..." Again, more fumbling. "This is really lovely. Right now. In this moment." He smiles. Genuine and open and honest and happy and okay with me. He hugs me again, holds me close. That throbbing cock against me, causing more pangs of desire right where it needs to go.

"Okay," is all he says. "Do you want me to keep going, or...maybe we can just...hang out?" His eyes are genuinely concerned for me. I didn't even cry. Just welled-up a little. It's really endearing.

"I want you. Again. Now," is what I tell him. To put a period on the whole thing, my hands go to the base of his shaft, begin cradling everything. "I want this cock. I want your cum in me."

His arms swoop around my back, unhooking my bra in an assured motion. Any emotion from before has morphed, and we're full on making out, my leg raised so he can get even closer to me. We're pawing animals. He's holding on to my breast, teasing and sucking my achingly hard nipples. His hard-on throbs in my hand, and I'm moaning in his ear as he returns the favor, his hand finding my sopping cunt and rubbing at the lips.

"You're soaking," he tells me. It just sets me off and I tremble.

"Just fuck me, please! Fuck my pussy!" A husky moan into his ear. I like my dirty talk, like how out of breath I am and how it seems to drive him wild.

I know I'm no tiny Tara, so I'm very impressed that Mark is able to lift me up by my ass – I let out a very silly and shocked squeal - until I'm sliding myself over his cock, my legs instinctively wrapped tightly around him. I'm not touching the ground anymore, stuck between his rock hard cock and the wall.

Entering me with such force is something brand new, sparks blasting behind my eyes. If I thought he was deep before, I didn't know what I was thinking.

"Oh fuck, oh fuck, oh fuck," I can't help but say, louder and quicker with each thrust as he goes in and out. I'm so wet, he's gliding with ease.

Faster and faster. I can feel my ass bouncing, my chest heaving. He's starting to tense up, his arm muscles pulling tight. As sure a sign as ever.

"Fill me up. Fill me up. I want it baby. Fill my cunt!" I exclaim. He nods, grunting. One of my hands pressed against his abs, the other one clinging on to his shoulder. All this pressure building, all things about to go. As he comes, I feel my own orgasm unleash over him too. He moans into me, one final push as his cock lets loose in me, gives me what I needed.

The sounds I make, tight little screams that overwhelmed his orgasmic sigh, echo through the empty pizzeria.

"Holy shit," I say, stunned, disbelief over what I just felt. He gently places me down, and we both try to regain our senses. He collapses into me, both of us supporting ourselves against the wall. Flushed and warm and glowing and happy.

If you had told me when I started at ClassSeven all those months ago that it would lead to some of the best sex in my life - at 2AM in a closed-down pizzeria - I would have thought you were crazy.

CHAPTER 13 – MARK

TIME PASSES. MORE days and weeks. Hot summer ones. There's light at the end of the tunnel for time being, at least when it comes to ClassSeven and this app we're building. We're close to launching, close to the last phase of marketing. Close to finishing this contract.

Talking with Anna made me realize so many things about the company. Conversations over some wine and movies at her place. She was open and honest and cut right to the heart of the matter. Brazenly so. Severe in her truth-telling. I still appreciated it.

"You look burnt out, sometimes," she says. "You can't just move into this app idea you have." I had told her I didn't want to take another freelance contract for the company, but instead, wanted to build our own thing. "Take a vacation. Everyone should." She talks about her trip to Morocco a few years prior. It wasn't exactly relaxing - "I ran around, trying to see everything I could" - but it still helped. "It'll help you too. You're young yet. Take a month."

It's a lot of advice to chew on, and something tells me I'm only scratching the surface of her intelligence, but it makes sense in the end.

I take Sean and Cody out to lunch one day, the sun fully out for a wonderful day. Over burgers, I tell them that there'll be vacation time first – ClassSeven will be able to afford everyone geeing some paid time off - and then we'll be working on the app I had pulling at my brain earlier. I pitched it to them.

We built ClassSeven in a tiny apartment, already a success before the investors. Nothing's a guarantee though, and I was nervous thoughout the whole spiel. I felt relieved and lucky as they accepted it for what it was. We excitedly chit-chatted about what we have to do to make the dream a reality, what we could do to keep ClassSeven going even further down the line

Anna won't give me an answer about coming on full time. My feelings about that oscillate. On one hand, I want to be around her a lot more. On the other, it's her choice, and unseen issues may arise. Since that night in the pizzeria, we've been seeing each other much more frequently. Almost every night that we can. I don't want to spoil it.

We've been keeping it incredibly professional at the office. Not even a hint that anything might be different. The breakup gossip is enough to keep Cody, Sean and Caitlin going in our little circle. With that little cloud hanging over my head – one that, granted, is fading by the day – I don't want anyone to even get an inkling about Anna and I. I don't watch the videos Tara's made, but I know they're out there. I know that people are far too involved in my love-life at the moment. No more fuel for that fire.

With the pizzeria apartment needing some renovations, I've been splitting my time between some hotels and Anna's place. I prefer her place over anything. It feels inviting, and warm, and has her personality spread all over it. It's endearing and I get some of the best sleeps of my life there.

In the morning light, I can take the time to admire every inch of her. All her curves. Her thick thighs, her ample assets. The dimples on her lower back. The way her hair falls about her and seems completely untamed. Her smile, wide and promising. My favorite thing to do is wrap my arms around her, push my hard cock against her leg while she's sleeping. Feel her up as she rouses from her slumber, always willing for more. Turning over and kissing me, pulling me close.

We'll whisper sweet nothings, greet the day in the throes of passion. Falling, body and soul. I love that it's becoming our normal.

CHAPTER 14 – ANNA

TODAY WILL BE MY LAST day at ClassSeven. My contract's done, the app is successfully on it's way, and the office is temporarily closing next week for everyone to get some vacation time. I still haven't thought about joining full time. I probably won't, which I think will make Mark a little sad. He accepts it though, a knock on the chin he can deal with.

"I guess you wouldn't want to get sick of me," he mentions one night as we wait for our Thai takeout to finish cooking. Just the most completely adorable boyfriend in shorts and bright, loose t-shirt. "Too much of a good thing." He winks, and it makes me roll my eyes sarcastically.

It's so sweet, and he's so accepting. It's hard not to feel too conflicted about anything as we spend more time together. Hell, we're even going to take a little trip while he's off. That's what matters most these days, the moments we're together. I kiss his cheek.

Dating Mark just happened naturally. Less time making out and doing vulgar things to each other. More time chatting, getting food, and napping together. There's still that overpowering lust – sometimes I just stare at him at work, thinking of how closing the door to his office and ravaging him would be the best alternative to answering emails – but we're more than that these days. He's got a drive and verve that a lot of guys I dated previously didn't have. He makes me laugh. There's still that reserved nature about him. The deep pool of his confidence marred with a black tar of consistent self-consciousness. Still, I live for him to smile.

I do notice the people behind the food counter giving us a suspicious look as I kiss him and they hand our food to us. I'm dealing with the age difference and some of the more judgemental stares it gets. I told my mom over video chat that I was dating a younger man, and even though she didn't make any comments, her stone face when I gave her the news was very similar to one I received when I was caught drinking in high-school.

No one at ClassSeven knows yet. Mark's still dealing with some Tara stuff and wants any privacy he can get. Her videos bitching about him stopped, and the condo stopped appearing, but Sean and Cody think he's crazy for breaking up with her.

"Why, man!? She's so hot!" Sean told him one time, well within earshot of me. Mark just shrugged and tried to play it cool.

"Better things came along," he tells them, not even looking up from his phone. I pretended to ignore them, acting like I was just working casually, but my heart was doing somersaults. I could have smooched him in front of all of them right there. A big, cartooney smacker right on the lips.

I made sure I treated him right later that night, and in the sticky warmth of our bed, I told him if they bumped into us on the street, there wouldn't be any mistake. I like having my hand in his back pocket, giving his butt a sweet little squeeze as we go about our business. A little show-off, I guess.

"I'll cross that bridge when I get to it," he says. "It's low on the totem pole of concerns at the moment."

All of that leading to my last day. The future is open, but I'm happy to have Mark be a part of it. He'll be taking me out for a nice business lunch, but I have a feeling everyone in the office will join us for it. No private date, but that's just something to deal with, to shrug off and move on.

Even with all that, I can't find the energy to get out of bed at the moment. There's a ding from my phone – a text from Mark – that forces my hand, makes me wake up and get moving. I figure it's about some work stuff, and I delay checking it until after my shower. I'm glad I get a look at it though.

Don't wear panties today.

It feels naughty, a dare I'm sure he's planned out very carefully. Maybe when everyone else is gone, he'll go down on me as I straddle that terrible eyesore of a foosball table. Maybe he'll come on his desk again, and let me lick it up for him. Maybe he just wants to tease me. All these possibilities.

It is what it is, and that's that. It's my future.

About the Author

Elizabeth Walker is a writer based near Toronto, Canada.